Tru
Ones

By   Jaleen Collins

ISBN: 979-8-218-00332-6

DEDICATION

I dedicated this book to my grandmother Velvet love. I also dedicate this book to my family and friends for always believing in my vision. My mom Lisa Collins thank you for always guiding me on the right path and pushing me to be great.To Karla my girlfriend thank you for pushing me to accomplish something that I've always wanted.To my dad Rashawn Collins thank you for understanding that I have a bigger purpose in life than basketball and allowing me to chase after something much greater.To my brother Rob I want to truly say thank you because without you this book wouldn't exist from thing you showed from superheroes all the way to science fiction. My friends Terrell and Juniah I consider y'all to be my best friends y'all have never gave up on my vision and for that I am eternally grateful forever. To my bro Justin thank you for always telling me to keep going. To Quay thank you for always giving me the greatest advice through this stressful process letting me know it will pay off soon.
Truly love you all. Some may not know but every single one of you guys had a big part in this book.
Thank you.

Table of contents

ACKNOWLEDGMENTS

I want to take the time before you get into reading this body of work I have
prepared for you. I want you as the reader to know and always and
remember whatever you want to do in life do it and don't do it partially.
Give it your all and do what makes you happy.
I spent years of going through multiple drafts of this book until I literally
said I'm going to do this the way I want to. Not caring what any says and
just doing this straight from the heart.

Dream a better Future and make it happen.

This book is 7 years in the making.

And now I give to you TRU ONES.

Tru Ones

Chapter 1:Prologue

In the year 1990, an African American scientist named Bernard Robinson worked under the lead scientist, an African American man by the name of Zion Pierce, at GenX Tech. This secret facility works with research to find possible new discoveries within the human genome and Create technology for the government and military. The 2 of them work in the particular project division of GenX Tech. The unique project division is where the United States government tests new weapons, vehicles, aircraft, and new tech for the military. The facility was filled with computers and high-tech features.

One day Nasa got an alert that something had entered the atmosphere. The U.S government contacted them to tell them that the object landed 80 miles northwest of them in the Grand Canyon. Zion began to gather a team of soldiers to explore the crash site. Zion arrives at the crash with his squad, anxious about what they might find. They look around and see a trail of flames burning and smoke within the red rock of the hot desert. Zion begins to follow the path that would lead them to the crash site. They arrive at the scene where they find themselves standing in front of a crater the size of 3 houses and smoke. Zion signals the team to go in the smoke and see what is there.

"I'm not going over there. I didn't sign up for this man." Said one of the soldiers to Zion.

Zion looks over at him, walks over to him, and says. "Last time I checked, I was the boss." Trying to intimidate the soldier. The soldier replies to Zion by nodding his head and saying yes, sir."Now go over there and do what I told you," says Zion. The troops start moving in the smoke and wave their weapons around to clear the fog. As the smoke begins to remove, a body begins to become visible. It's a being that looks to be human with hieroglyphics imprinted on its skin. The soldier all look in shock.

"How's it going in there, boys?" He yells to the team.

"It's a person over here, Mr. Pierce," said one of the soldiers.

"Really? Well, are they breathing?" he asks the group.

The soldiers move closer and poke the being with their guns to see if it is alive. The being awakens and defends himself thinking he's being attacked. Gunshots start to go off within the smoke.

"What's going on in there?" Zion wonders and asks them.The being grabs a soldier and then chops him in the neck. He rushes another, grabs him, and throws him 15 feet away from the smoke. The being jumps out of the smoke, surprising everyone in sight. Towering at 8ft tall with light brown skin.

"Shoot him! Now!" yells Zion Pierce at his team.

The soldiers load and aim their weapons and point at the being. The being puts his hand up and creates a shield out of thin air. The bullets come in contact with protection and stick to it. He then points the security up towards the sky, fires the shot into the air, and explodes the bullets like fireworks. Everybody screams out in fear except for Zion. The being slowly levitates off the ground and sniffs the air as he rises off the ground.

"I can't recognize this planet at all," the being as he speaks.

"You're on the planet Earth. Why is it that you look human?" He then asks the alien being.

"This is what Earth looks like now. I can't believe this. Earth used to be a beautiful place worldwide animals all around people all around what happened?" the being wonders to himself, speaking out loud.

He then hovers down towards Zion and Towers over him, glaring.

Zion signals the team to take him down. The soldier shoots tranquilizers at him and captures and takes him to the facility.

Zions team gets back to GenX Tech with the being.

"Okay, let's unload the boys and put him in a room. I've got some questions to ask him," he says to his team.

Bernard walks over to the loading, figuring out what is going on. "Who is that guy Pierce?" Asked Bernard.

"We're about to find out in just a little bit because I've got some questions to ask him," Zion replies.

Bernard grabs Zion's arm, trying to stop him, and says. "I don't think this a good idea, man."

He looks at Bernard and says. "We need to know who or what he is and why he is here?" Zion pulls his arm away from Bernard and begins to walk away.

In the interrogation room, The being is strapped down.

Zion opens the door, walks into the room with a chair, takes a seat, and says. "Now, let's talk!"

The being just looks at Zion with no emotion. And begins to speak in Swahili.

What are you speaking about? Asks Zion.

"I said my name is Saijin Clarivet," as he addresses Zion in English.

Zion looks up in shock at Saijin and then begins to chuckle. He then says to him. "So you do understand what I'm saying, good. Why are you here, and are there more like you?"

Saijin Clarivet breaks free from what is holding him down

"If you're wondering if I'm a threat, I'm not, and I don't remember how I crashed down to this planet," Says Saijin, standing there in front of Zion, free of the shackles restraining him.

"This planet is called earth," says Zion writing stuff on his clipboard

"I've been here before a long time ago. It was such a beautiful place before with huge amounts of animals and nature; what happened?" Asked Saijin, slowly pacing around the room, confused about what happened to him.

"I don't know. Now, why is it that you look human, Saijin? And what are those tattoos?" Asked Zion sitting there staring at his tattoos.

"There's a lot of things you humans are not aware of, and these are the markings from a warrior branch across the cosmos," Says Saijin.

"We're going to run some test on your blood," Says Zion as he stands up and walks up to Saijin Clairvet and looks him in the eye, and Zion walks out of the room.

They begin to start testing the blood and find out that Saijin blood is the rarest and most dangerous blood in the world Rh null with a mixture of AB-negative never seen before.

"That can't be right; he's human," Zion mentions as he smiles at the lab results.

Zion walks into the room where Saijin is.

"You look similar to us because you're human?" Ask Zion, confused at the results.

"Yes, I am, but you won't understand," they replied to Zion.

Zion tells Saijin. He then tells Saijin. "You're going to help us out and get me to understand. We're going to need a lot of your blood."

"What does that mean?" Saijin says to Zion.

"Don't worry, nothing bad," Zion smiles and replies to Saijin

Later on, Zion talks to Bernard about creating a serum from Saijin blood

"That sounds insane; how do we know if it will work?" Bernard asks

He tells Bernard trying to convince him. "We don't, but we will run the test until we get it. This can be the future for the military to think about it. Enhanced soldiers nationwide can save families from losing their children. We can also cure so many diseases and illnesses on the planet.""It's hazardous, but we might have a chance to pull it off with the proper science," he replies to Zion, interested in the experiment to see what happens.

"That's it; let's get moving on it," Zion responded to Bernard, excited about possibly making a new discovery.

They work on the serum for weeks and test it out and fail.

"It feels as if we're never going to get this down, man," he's to Zion, frustrated about the project.

"We just have to keep working on it, so make some tweaks and do another test," he tells him, being hopeful.

"Hey, Dr. Pierce, there's a phone call for you," says one other scientist.

"Okay, coming; tell them to give me one moment," He then walks to the phone and picks it up.

"Hello, this is officer Trevor. Is this Zion Pierce, the older brother of Adrain Pierce?" Asked Officer Trevor standing in the precinct.

"Yeah, is everything okay?" Asks Zion standing at the phone, worried.

"Umm, No, Sir, I'm very sorry to say this Adrain was involved in a traffic stop. He wasn't cooperating and resisted arrest and was put down by one of our officers," The officer says to Zion, sitting down at his desk and rubbing his head.

"Where is my brother?" Asks Zion beginning to get angry over the phone.

Officer Trevor says to Zion. "I know this might be hard to process."

"You Put my brother down like he's some type of dog. Are you serious!" he starts yelling at officer Trevor.

Moments later, Zion just sitting in his office, and Bernard walks in there. He sees Zion sitting there looking at a picture of his Brother and drinking some whiskey as tears begin to fall onto the picture he's holding in his hands.

"Pierce, you okay, man?" Asked Bernard, concerned about him, as he saw Zion just sitting there.

"No, I don't think I will be either," he says to Bernard as he takes a gulp of the whiskey on his desk.

"They killed my little brother; he was a good kid, and I will avenge him," He Tells Bernard as he looks back down at the picture of his brother again, crying and trying to speak as his voice is breaking.

"Everyone will pay, and We need to finish that serum right now," he says to him with the tone of revenge.

"No, man, you need time to grieve; we can worry about that serum later," he responds to Zion and walks over to him and takes the whiskey from him.

"I need to finish this. Just know this serum is no longer for the military, and this serum will be for our people!" he angrily shouts at Bernard and stands up and looks him in the face.

"What are you talking about, Pierce?" Asked Bernard confused at what Zion was talking about.

"Don't you get tired of walking around in fear of where to go and where not to go," he says to Bernard.

"Yeah, I get tired of it, but this isn't the way. I know you're angry, but revenge is never the answer," he tells Zion.

"This serum can level the playing field where no black woman, man, or child has to live in fear. We can take control and be in charge, not them," He yelled at Bernard in his face.

"Zion, think about what you are saying," he begins yelling back at Zion."They killed my brother. I will make all of them pay, and Bernard, I am thinking of a better future," Zion says firmly to Bernard.

"I won't be a part of this. I refuse; this is not what we started this project for," Bernard replies and begins to walk away.

Zion walks out of the office to the lab to look at the testings

"Bernard, can you hear me?" Saijin starts whispering to Bernard, communicating telepathically.

"Who are you, and how are you doing that?" Bernard questions Saijin.

"I need you to help me; Zion's plan is full of pure rage and revenge; we need to get out of here," Saijin tells Bernard.

"Why should I trust you?" Bernard asks him.

"I read his mind; he wants to become the one with all the power and control, not give it back," Saijin replies to Bernard.

Zion walks into the lab and looks for the serum.

"What are you doing, Dr. Pierce? Stop what you're doing; this isn't a good idea; we haven't even started human testing," One of the scientists says to Zion.

"Well, I'm going to do the honor and become the first," he says as he injects himself with the serums and starts to have a reaction.

Bernard runs to the room where Saijin is being held in.

"Come on, let's get out of here," Bernard says as he Breaks the door open.

Saijin Gets up, and they leave the room with Bernard as the alarm starts to go off throughout the building.

"Bernard, What's happening?" Saijin asks Bernard as they start to run to the lab.

"You can't go in there, Bernard." Says the lady scientist to Bernard.

"Why, what happened?" Bernard asks the lady as she panics.

"I don't know what happened, but Zion injected himself with serum," Says the lady scientist to Bernard.

"This was the plan you talked about him doing right," Bernard looks over at Saijin.

He looks up at Bernard and says, "Yes, this is exactly what I saw."

Bernard looks at the other scientists and asks, "Many more samples are there?"

"There's like 8 more serum samples of the one he injected himself in there," Says the lady scientist to him.

"Okay, I'm going to get them," he replies to The Scientist.

"Wait, you don't know what that serum just did to him. We have to get out of here," Saijin says to Bernard.

"Not without those samples," he looks at Saijin, runs into the lab, and starts to grab the samples.

"Put them down, Bernard," Zion Stands up with his back turned to Bernard and turns around, and his eyes are red with a gray stream in the front of his hair.

"Zion, the serum, what did it dot you?" Bernard asks Zion looking at him, terrified.

"What was needed to bring order to this country?" Zion snarls to Bernard and starts walking towards Bernard, and Bernard throws chairs and shelves down and runs.

"We have to go right now." Like now.

"Okay," Saijin replies to Bernard as he sees A chair gets thrown out the lab window.

"What the hell was that?" Bernard asks him in fear.

"Bernard, hand me those samples now!" He then starts to yell.

"Run!" Bernard screams to Saijin out of fear to get out of the facility with the Serums.

Bernard and Saijin run to the hangar and get in one of the helicopters. The facility is going into lockdown.

"Alright, get in!" Bernard says to Saijin as they get ready for take-off, and Zion runs in the hangar, trying to disrupt their take-off.

"You're not going anywhere! Now give me the samples right now," he jumps on board the helicopter, attempting to steal the serums back.

"We're not giving you anything," Saijin says to that Zion as he closes his eyes, and gold dust appears and creates a staff in plain sight.

"What the hell did you just do?" Zion asks Saijin as he looks at him, baffled.

Saijin hits Zion with the staff, causing him to fly off the helicopter to the ground.

"What happened? Is Zion gone? How did you do that?" Bernard asks, amazed by what Saijin just did with his hands.

"It is one of the many gifts I possess; it's called Imagination creation. By achieving a total state of Consciousness, you can create anything in front of you. I haven't mastered it yet; actually, it takes a lot of training and practice to obtain that skill level," Saijin explains to Bernard as they look at him, shocked by what he can do.

The 2 of them reach an off-the-grid location where they discuss their plan for the vials of blood.

Bernard decides to open a facility where he can safely hide the vials of Saijin blood, and they begin to create more weapons, equipment, and vehicles.

"This is definitely the most necessary precaution for the future because I know that Zion will come for that blood one day and bring a reckoning," Saijin speaks to Bernard about the future he fears is coming.

"I know we're hiding the serums, but what should we do with it?" He then says to him, asking about the plan for the future.

"Hide it within the heart of the next generation, the bodies of the next generation. Trust me, you'll know when the time is right for it, "Saijin says to him.

Bernard shrugs his shoulders and looks down at the vials of the serums.

"Now, I must depart from you, Bernard," he tells him.

"Wait, where are you going?" he looks at him as he gets ready to leave him.

"I can't say, but just know I will meet one day again. I'm pursuing something great out there," Saijin replies to Bernard.

Saijin flies off into the sky, and with a loud boom, he breaks the sound barrier and vanishes into the atmosphere.

Bernard closes the vials of the serum into a vault inside his facility. Begins to walk to the exit of his building, turns the lights, and walks out the door.

Bernard started to spend more time with his family and grandchildren, Robert Champion and Jalen Collins. Robert was 10 years old already, and Bernard began to spend more time with him and make up for the lost amount of time. Jalen was a baby about 8 months old that started to get sick. Jalen was diagnosed with moderate persistent asthma that caused him to have symptoms every day. Bernard heard began to start running tests on Jalen's blood and his oxygen levels. Bernard finds out that serum can boost his oxygen levels and blood proteins. Bernard tests Jalen's blood with the serum, which unites his cells and makes them stronger. Bernard concludes that he is going to use them on serum on Jalen. Bernard gets one of the serums and injects it into Jalen. Jalen's oxygen level rise, and the asthma is gone from his system. Bernard smiles but also worries now for the day that Zion comes for the serums and possibly Jalen now.

Chapter 2

15 years later

"Alright does everyone have the notes for today before we move on to the next thing?" asks Mr. Martin as he stands in front of his desk with his arm folded.

Mr. Martin looks around the class at all the students

"Yo Jae, wake up, dude; he's looking around," Justin Whispers to Jalen and balls a piece of paper up and throws it at Jalen to wake him up.

"Look alive, Mr. Jalen!" Mr. Martin Yells across the classroom so Jalen can hear him.

"Dang welp, I tried, man," Justin says.

Jalen jumps up out of his sleep.

"I wasn't sleeping!" Jalen says aloud to the class as he jumps up from his sleep.

The class then starts to laugh at Jalen.

"Well, if you weren't sleeping, Mr. Jalen, then where are all your notes?" Mr. Martin chuckles and asks Jalen.

"Well, actually, that's a great question because I don't even know, so yeah, you got me," Jalen looks up and says to Mr. Martin.

"Really, a dude, come on," Mr. Martin shakes his head and begins to take a seat at his desk.

The bell rings for the end of the class period, and everybody gathers all their stuff to exit the classroom.

"Enjoy the rest of your day, everybody!" Mr. Martin says to the class as he leans back in his chair.

"Jalen, you mind if I talk to you for a quick second?" Mr. Martin asks Jalen before he walks out of the class.

"Aye, Justin, I'll catch up with you in a little bit, bro," Jalen says to Justin as he stops in front of Mr. Martin's desk.

"Okay, bro, I'll just be out here in the hallway waiting for you," Justin tells Jalen standing in the classroom doorway.

Mr. Martin stands up to talk to Jalen, and he stands across from him, leaning on his desk with his hands in his pants pockets. "Jalen, look, man, I can't keep letting you slide because you're on the basketball team. I think you're a kid with a lot of potentials. Come on, man, you're the captain of the robotics club; how are you so lazy. You know that's not going to cut it in the real world."

Jalen begins to sit on one of the desktops.

Jalen asks, "Mr. Martin, why are you telling me all of this?"

"Jalen, all I'm saying is I want you to apply yourself more because I know you can be the best student in my class, that's it," he said to Jalen as they both stood in front of the desks face to face.

"Okay, I got you, Mr. Martin. I will try and do better," Jalen tells Mr. Martin.Mr. Martin says to Jalen and softly hits him on his shoulder. "Alright, now get out of here, kid, and don't forget to tell coach jones about the robotics competition on Wednesday; we need you."

"I'll see you tomorrow, Mr. Martin," Jalen tells Mr. Martin as he walks out of the classroom.

Outside the classroom, Justin stands there waiting for Jalen to talk to Brea and Maya, and Jalen freezes as soon as he comes out of the school where he sees Maya. Jalen becomes at a loss for words to see his crush standing out there with her ponytail and brown skin looking great in Jalen as it shines from the sunlight.

"Oh, what's up, Jalen?" Maya smiles and says to Jalen.

"Damn, finally, what took so long, Jae?" Justin asks Jalen.

"Maya, what's up? How are you? Mr.Martin just wants me to apply myself more in his class," he said to them all.

"Okay, cool, nothing major to really worry about," Justin says to Jalen and starts to laugh.

"Yeah, I'm good, though; Jalen is just ready for the weekend to start, honestly," She tells him as he walks up in front of Maya.

"Wait, are you going to the game Friday?" He asks Maya hoping she says yes.

She looks and smiles at Jalen and says, "I'm not sure, honestly."

He says to her. "Come on, this is one of our biggest games of the season, and you could help Justin lead the student section to cheer us on; we need all the support."

Brea grabs Maya's arm and says, "No, Maya, we're going to go; we don't have anything better to do Friday."

Jalen puts his hands up and says. "Alright, sounds cool, actually."

"Maya, be prepared to lose your voice in the student section," Justin says to her because it's the first game she's coming to.

"Well, I'm going to be cheering but not screaming," she replies to him and laughs.

"Justin, you're going to save us some spots, right?" Brea asks Justin.

"Yeah, I'll try; it's gonna be packed that night but just try to get here on time," he says to her, responding about saving seats.

"Alright, so what's everyone doing for winter break?" Jalen then asks all of them.

"Well, I'm going somewhere; my parents always want to make a family trip on winter break. I think they said we are going to Florida to the amusement parks down there," Brea responds to Jalen about winter break.

"Jae, you already know I have to drive up to boring-ass Virginia to see family there," Justin also responds with his plans.

"Bro, it's really not even that bad come on, dude," Jalen says to him and laughs.

He then tells Jalen, Brea, and Maya how much he doesn't like going to Virginia." Jae, I literally have no cousins my age, at least guy cousins. I have like two girl cousins my age, and they're annoying. My guy cousins are all five or six years younger; they're still in elementary school."

"Are you still going to bring your game system to your grandparents' house?" He then asks him.

"Dude, I forgot to tell you the worst part about going there this time; my grandparents got rid of the router; they have just straight cable TV," he says to Jalen.

"Damn, that truly sucks because you're going to be so bored there," he says to Justin, and they all start to laugh at him.

"Dude, please do not remind me I'm really not ready for this at all, bro; that's not funny, come on," he replies to Jalen, chuckling and smacking him lightly."Yeah, Jae, he's right; that's not funny. Justin, wait for one more thing real quick; you better download some movies and get some board games to keep yourself occupied," Maya laughed. Jalen and brea begin to join in and laugh with her.

"Alright, enough about my winter break; what are you two doing for the break this year?" he asks Jalen and Maya about their plans.

"Well, you already know I'm doing the same thing I usually do. I will be here stuck in Georgia," she looks at them all and replies to Justin.

"Dang, you too, I'm going to be here bored this whole break," he then replies to Justin's question after hearing Maya's answer.

"Wait, you're going to be here for the break; that's cool; that's not cool, but you know what I mean," Maya replies to Jalen, trying to be nonchalant.

Justin and brea look at each other and laugh at how awkward Jalen and Maya are.

"What are y'all laughing at?" Jalen asks Justin and Brea, so confused about what's going on.

"Jae, it's nothing, don't worry," Brea replied to him and still laughed at them.

"I have to go see coach real quick. I'm going to just catch y'all after the game tonight," Jalen says to all of them.

"Alright, bet, bro," Justin and Jalen do their handshake.

"Wait, guys, what time does the game start again?" Brea asks Justin and Jalen.

"It starts at 8, right Jae?" He asks Jalen.

"Yeah, bro, it starts at 8pm; no, wait; actually, it's at 730. I believe just check the school website it would tell you; Honestly, I think it starts at 730," Jalen replies to them, unsure of the correct time of the game."Brea, what time do you want to come to get me from my house, or should I just come to your house?" Maya looks over and asks Brea.

"I'll just come over around at like five o'clock; we could just chill out for a while and get ready around like six o'clock,"

"Alright, that sounds like a good plan," Said Maya to brea.

"Hold on, you two think y'all will get ready in an hour," Justin then says to Brea and Maya.

"Honestly, it's not me; it's this girl right here, Maya; she's probably going to try to put her make-up on and stuff," Brea says as she laughs at Maya.

"I don't know why I think you look better without it, just natural you, and some lip gloss looks good to me," he then said to Brea about how he views Maya.

Maya looks up at Jalen and smiles at him, and Justin looks up at Jalen in shock at what he just said.

"Wait, I just said that out loud, didn't I? Well, I think I'm going to go ahead go now; see y'all later," Jalen realizes what he said and is embarrassed. He begins to walk away from them.

"I was not expecting him to say that at all," Brea was shocked at what Jalen said.

"I'm surprised too. I didn't know Jae felt that way," Maya is also shocked.

"Maya, really, you never knew. The way you two are always looking at each other. You guys' awkward conversations have made it completely obvious that you like him too," Justin stands there and tells Maya.

"Brea, wow, you told Justin; how could you?" Maya gets upset with Brea.

"Wait, what did I do?" Brea answered, super confused."Brea didn't say anything; it's obvious we all see how you look at him all bubbly, Like just tell him because he does not think you do," Justin responds to Maya.

"Why does he think I don't like him? I've had a crush on him for the last 3 or 4 years now," she said to him about Jalen.

"It's because he's Jae that's the simplest answer I could give you. The wait is that the reason you decline Derrick asking you to homecoming earlier in the school year and Jordan last year as well," he says, questioning Maya.

"Yeah, I was waiting for Jalen to ask me both times to homecoming, but he didn't even try. He's one of my best friends. I thought he would have caught on, but of course, not Jalen is really in his own world sometimes. Oh, I told Jordan no because he wanted to get at Jalen. Yeah, he was just trying to piss him off because he knows Jalen would probably be mad at me for going with him; quote " mortal enemy," she says to Justin and Brea.

"Okay, Friday is your chance to finally make a move for sure or for him to make," she said to Maya.

"Justin can you do me a favor and get him to make a move on me because it would be pretty cool for us to hang out on winter break," she simply asks him.

"I will definitely try to give him hints that he definitely needs to," he replies to her.

Jalen walks up to Coach jones's office and knocks on the door.

"What's up, Jae? Come in, man?" Coach jones tells Jalen as he knocks on the door."Aye, what's up, coach?" he replies and begins to walk in and sits down in front of coach jones.

"What on your mind, kid?" Coach simply asks Jalen."Nothing really. I just wanted to come and tell you I won't be able to make practice Wednesday because of the robotics club," he said to Coach Jones.

"Damn, really, it was a couple of things I really wanted you to see in practice on Wednesday. I drew up a new play for you; it's really a late-game situation play," he says to Jalen.

"My bad, coach, but if you have a copy of the play, I could read over it, and you know it doesn't take me to get a play right," he smiles and tells him.

"Alright, the man sounds good to me. Tomorrow at practice, I'll give you a copy, so go home and chill, man," he laughs and tells Jae.

"Alright, I will see you later, Coach," he says to his coach as he gets up and fist bumps him, and walks out of his office.

Jalen walks down the hallway, takes his backpack off his back, searches for the keys to his car, takes his phone out of his pocket, and texts Justin, Brea, and Maya.

"Jae just texted us if we want some egg rolls?" Justin tells Brea and Maya as he looks down at his phone. "You know I can always go for some egg rolls from Rob's and let Jae know we will meet him there," Brea replies to Justin.

Brea, Maya, and Justin all begin to walk out of the school and get in the car and leave the school grounds to meet Jalen and get something to eat.

Jalen begins to walk to his car while listening to his music. Jalen gets in his car, tosses his backpack into the passenger seat, and turns his car on. The noise of the engine goes Vroom in a thunderous tone.

"Oh yeah, let's go get something to eat now because I'm super hungry," Jalen says as he texts Justin that he's about to leave the school.

Jalen leaves the school parking lot and takes off down the road.

Brea, Maya, and Justin arrive at the restaurant Let's Roll'up, which has different egg rolls. They walk in and sit down at a table.

Rob walks over to the table. He is the owner of the restaurant and also Jalen's older brother.

"What's up, everybody ?" Rob to them.

"Yeah, we just got out of school, and we waiting on Jae; he should be here any moment." Justin then responds to him.

"Alright, cool, Justin, I got a new spicy sauce; you wanna try it?" Rob replies back to Justin.

"Is that a challenge because you know I'm going to try it?" Justin questions Rob.Jalen walks into the restaurant, walks over to the table, and Daps up.

"What's good, bro? You Alright?" Robs asks Jalen.

"Yeah, I'm cool. I'm just hungry like I'm starving," Jae responds to his brother as he begins to sit down at the table next to Maya, and the two look at each and smile. Brea picks up the menu and looks at it.

"You guys think y'all know what you're going to get because I think I'm ready?" Brea says to Justin,

Maya, and Jalen while Rob is still at the table to take their order.

Jalen takes a quick glance at the menu and tells Rob. "Yeah, I think I'm ready, Rob."

"Jae, you want the plant-based meat egg roll today?" Rob asked Jalen if that's what he wanted.

"Is it actually good because it sounds kinda good?" Maya looks at Rob and Jae and asks both of them.

"Yeah, it's actually pretty good. I like it and If you don't want to be healthy, try it out," Rob tells Maya as he chuckles.

"Okay, I think I'm going to try it out," Maya says as she smiles and hands rob her menu.

"Yo Rob, I think I'm ready for your challenge," Justin says to rob and looks over.

"Alright, all I can tell you is that it's hot as hell, and It's called flaming habanero; you think you can handle it?" Rob says to him, hyped up for him to try the new sauce.

"Yeah, I got it. I accept the challenge, and I want it with shrimp inside," Justin looks over at Rob and begins to chuckle.

"Okay, Rob, I want the buffalo chicken roll with onion rings," Brea tells rob as she gives her menu to him.

Rob walks back to the kitchen with their orders taken down on a notepad.

Some time passes at the restaurant, and rob walks out of the kitchen to bring their food.

"Here's all of y'all food, man, and I got some fried rice coming out too," Rob tells them all as he begins to set the food down on the table.

"Bro, this looks so good right now," Jalen says as he looks up at Rob and fist bumps him; the two begin to chuckle.

"I don't know about y'all, but I'm digging in on this food. I'm hungry," Brea says as she takes her first bite into her buffalo chicken roll.

"Exactly, they're not hungry for real, I think," Maya replies to Brea as she begins to eat her food.

"Alright, rob, let's see what this shrimp roll talking about," Justin says to Rob before taking the first bite of the egg roll.

"What you think, man?" Rob replies to him as he witnesses him take his first bite.

"Aye, Rob, you might have something with this one," he says to rob as he looks over at him after enjoying his egg roll."Maya, how's the plant-based egg roll to you?" Jalen asks her as he looks across over at Maya.

"Okay, Rob, you really did your thing with this roll. I see why you get this one all the time, Jae," Maya replies to Jae after she enjoys her first bite of the egg roll.

Jae says to Maya. "See, I told you that junk is good; sometimes you just got to trust me," he smirks at her.

"Wait, Maya, does it actually taste like beef?" Rob asks Maya waiting for her response.

"Hold on, let me take another bite and think about it," she responds to rob as she starts giggling.

"It honestly tastes the same to me, but that's just me; everybody is different," Jae says to Rob and Maya as he eats his fries.

Maya starts taking a couple more bites from her egg roll and says. "It actually does taste the same. To be honest, it's not as heavy or greasy."

"That's why I sometimes eat it because I feel good afterward," Rob replies to Maya and Jae.

"Right after this, I got to go see grandpa, so rob, can I usually get his take over to him," Jae says to rob as he looks at the menu.

"Already got you covered; he actually called me earlier. Told me you were coming over later," Rob tells Jae as he cleans up his table.

"Damn, really, when did he call?" Jae asks Rob.

"His food should be done by now; let me go check on it," Rob replies to Jae as he begins to check in the kitchen if the food is done. Rob comes back out with the food in a bag. "Here you go, a little bit of everything should be in there, and I gave him onion rings and fries with it too," Rob tells Jae as he gives him the bag.

"Ight everybody ready to go," Justin asks everyone as he gets up from the table.

"Yeah, and full as hell, I think I need a nap after I drop y'all off," Brea says to them as she rubs her stomach.

"Bre, I felt that one because I'm so full too, and that was really good," she says, getting up and replying to Brea as she walks towards the exit.

"Justin, is brea taking you home, or are you riding with me to my grandpa's?" Jalen asks Justin as they walk out of the restaurant.

"Actually, I haven't seen your grandpa in a minute, so I'm going to ride with you," Justin simply replies to Jae.

"Ight bet that's cool with me," Jae says to Justin as they all begin to walk to their cars.

"Okay, we will see you guys later!" Brea says to Justin and Jalen. She walks up to her car, unlocks it, and opens the door, getting ready to get in.

"Jae, can you come here real quick?" Maya says to Jalen before she gets in the car.

Jalen starts to walk around to her and walks up to her. He then opens his mouth and says to her. "Yeah, what's up?"

"I'll see you later, Jae," Maya says to Jalen as she begins to step in to give him a really tight hug, then gets in the car.

Jalen stands there, blown away by her hugging him. Brea begins to reverse the car out of the parking spot.

"Damn, Jae, did she really just do that?" Justin asks Jalen if he stands on the side of Jalen's car.

"Dude, she really hugged me like I was not expecting that," Jalen says to Justin, still astonished.

Justin tells Jalen as they both begin to get in the car." Bro, she's basically giving you all the signs that she likes you. I keep telling you to go ahead and make a move; she's waiting on you for real. No one understands you better than that girl right there.""Bro, I know I just get nervous around her sometimes," Jalen says to Justin as he expresses himself while buckling up his seatbelt.

Justin begins laughing at Jalen. "Come on, man, all you have to do is just ask Maya out. We all know she's not going to say no to you. She always hinted at you to make a move, Brodie."

"Yeah, I'm going to, dude. I'm trying to figure out when to ask her for real," He says to him as he puts the keys in the ignition to start the car.

En begins to back out of the parking spot, and they both leave the parking lot.

"You know when you should ask her out?" Justin asks Jalen.

Jalen starts Laughing at Justin and tells him." Since you think you're such a pro. You think you're a ladies' man or something, bro. Go ahead, be my guest; tell me what you're going to suggest me to do."

"Okay, hear me out, so if we win on Friday, we'll probably go to rob's restaurant again. Y'all are most likely going chill and talk," said Justin to Jalen.

"Yeah, most likely is going to be the case if we win," he then said to Justin.

"See, you got to listen to your boy sometimes because I know, man," he tells him.

"Yeah, you know, a little bit, I'll give you that!" Jalen looks over and says to Justin quickly as they drive away to go to his grandpa's office.

Brea drives down the street, and she turns the music down in her car. Brea looks over and asks Maya. "Maya, what in the hell was that?"

"Honestly, I don't know. I was going to tell him something, then in my mind, I was like, go for a hug," Maya laughs as she tells brea.

"Yeah, when you hugged him, I was like, what is she doing," she says to Maya.

"He hugged me so tight I wasn't expecting that," Maya tells Brea as they drive down the street.

"I hope you finally stop playing around and just make it work while I'm gone on the whole winter break," she replies back to Maya as she continues down the street.

"Yeah, I hope, but there's no telling when he will build up the courage and finally do it," Maya says to Brea.

Brea laughs and says to Maya." I can't wait much longer. I will tell him to do it next time I see him. Everyone knows y'all like each other, just scared to take that step. I know Jalen likes you for sure because of that thing he said to you about make-up."

Maya responds to Brea." If you did that, he would be nervous immediately and start acting weird to me, so with that being said, don't do that. Hopefully, I can just spend a reasonable amount of time with him during the break."

Brea Starts laughing at what Maya previously said.

"Yeah, I think I will just tell him to stop acting like a punk," she says to Maya as she arrives at her house and pulls into the driveway.

Maya began to gather her stuff to get out of the car and said to her. "Brea, thanks for dropping me off. I'll see you in the morning." Maya then walks off from the car to go inside her house.

Brea then rolls her window and yells to Maya as she walks to her front porch." Tell your mom and sister I said hi because I haven't seen them in forever!"

She then backs out of Maya's driveway to leave and go home.

Jalen finally gets to his grandpa's office with Justin. They get out of the car, and Jalen reaches the back seat to get his grandpa's food. They walk up to the door and buzz the door to get into the building. (Buzzer sounds)

"Hello, who is it?" Grandpa says as he answers the door.

"Grandpa, it's me; Jae and I brought Justin too," he says as he leans into the doorbell mic.

"Okay, I'm letting you two in right now; hold on," he says to them both over the doorbell mic. (Buzzer sounds, and the clicks unlocked)

Jalen pulls the door open, and he and Justin begin to walk through the door. Jalen walks into Grandpa's office with the food from Rob's Restaurant in his hand.

Jalen knocks on the office door.

"Come on in, Jae," Grandpa Bernard says to Jalen after he knocks on the door.

"Okay!" he says as he opens the door and walks into Bernard's huge office.

Bernard gets up and walks over to both of them. He daps them both up and then says to them.

"What's up, guys? How was school feel like y'all learn anything new today?"

Jalen chuckles, and grandpa says. "Nothing, just another normal day of high school, honestly."

Justin chuckles as well and looks at Bernard, and says." Well, Jae fell asleep in class today."

"Dang, Justin, did you have to really say that?" Jalen says as he begins to shake his head.

"Jae, were you so tired that you took a little nap?" Grandpa Bernard says to Jalen, laughing.

"Not at all it's just when Mr. Martin does a presentation, he's turn the lights off, which makes me tired," Jalen explains to his Grandfather.

"Jae comes on, son, you can't fall asleep in class, man," Bernard says to his grandson.

"Yeah, grandpa, I know it's just that I already know this stuff about physics," Jae begins breaking down to grandpa about how he feels.

"Yeah, Jae, I understand I would have probably fallen asleep myself," Bernard begins to chuckle at Jalen.

"Yeah, honestly, we actually have more fun learning about science from you when we're here," Justin says to Bernard about science.

"Really, why is that the case?" Jae then responds to him.

"We do Experiments and tests a bunch of new materials when we're here, which makes it fun," Justin then says to them.

"Well, I feel like, in science, you need a hands-on experience to understand the basics," Bernard explains to both Jalen and Justin the fun science.

"With that being said, then grandpa, I want to work on some new things for the robotics club for the little robot fight on Wednesday," said Jalen to his Grandfather.

"Okay, kid, what'd you have in mind for some upgrades," Bernard says to Jae, curious about what Jae comes up with.

"There he goes about to start up the nerd stuff," Justin says as he starts laughing at Jalen.

"Wait, I'm confused. Didn't you just say that you think science is fun? Grandpa, you heard him say that right?" he responds to Justin after calling him a nerd.

"Yeah, I heard him for sure," Bernard says to Jalen about Justin."Yeah, let's not tell anybody about me saying that either. I don't want people to think I'm a science nerd," Justin replies to Jalen's Grandfather.

"Dude, there's really nothing wrong with being a nerd. You're just too worried about the perfect popular image you're trying to maintain," Jalen says to Justin about being a nerd.

"Jae, it's easier for you to say because you are the most popular guy in school, and you're considered the coolest nerd ever," Justin says to Jalen about him.

Bernard laughs at the two of them and begins to walk over to the desk, grabs his computer's desktop screen, and turns it around.

"Jae, would you want to do this with the robot design? Because if not, I got a couple more things that I think you might find interesting," Grandpa Bernard says to him about the robots.

Jalen walks over to the computer and sits down, and looks over. He clicks the computer mouse to go to the next screen and flips through a couple more designs that grandpa may have for him. Justin then sits down in a chair right next to Jalen.

"Honestly, grandpa, I love them all, so whenever you are ready. After going through the designs, I'm ready to get to work," he says.

He then begins to tell his grandson. "I was waiting for you to say that, kid. I'm gonna eat an egg roll, and right after that, we could get started. Is that good with you?" He then fists and bumps him.

"Hey Justin, you helping, bro, because this is gonna be fun for real?" he asks Justin out of curiosity as he and his Grandfather start to work on the designs.

"Umm, I actually don't know. I'm actually chilling right now, and I'm low-key tired," Justin replies to him about helping out."Oh, now you are tired, but you will be front and center, ready to help with our projects any other time. I think you just don't want to be doing nerdy stuff with us now because you're too cool for this," Bernard says while laughing at him.

"Okay, maybe a Lil bit, but you know I'm going to help; who cares what anybody says," Justin replies back to Bernard.

"Jae, can you go ahead and get the equipment? We nee out of the equipment room and take Justin because I'm sure we'll need a lot of things, man," he says to his grandson.

"Hold on really quick, Jae I'm going to let both parents know I might be home a little late," Justin says to Jalen as he takes his phone out of his pocket and starts texting his parents.

"All good, bro; take your time!" Jalen says to Justin as he starts to roll a cart to load the lab equipment they need to do their experiments.

Jalen walks into the lab room and starts to load stuff up when he stumbles over a box and falls. He picks up the package. He looks down and sees a sleeve hanging from the box.

Jalen reads the name on the box." Junk projects, what is all of this stuff?"

He then picks up a lightweight suit with a zipper in the back and inspects the suit from top to bottom, trying to figure out what it is.

Jalen glances at the suites he asks himself. "What the hell is this thing? It looks like some type of bodysuit?"

He then hears footsteps in the hallway, panics, and throws the suit into the lab cart. Justin walks into the equipment room and tries to scare Jalen.

"Boo!" Justin yells out to scare Jalen."Justin, did you speak to your parents about you being out a little late today," He then says to him nervously, trying to keep his cool about what he just found in that box.

"Dude, you good right now because you're acting on edge like you just saw something crazy or heard something?" Justin says to Jalen as he notices something is off with him.

"Yeah, bro, I'm fine; what makes you ask that?" he asks Justin, chuckling nervously.

"Okay, I'm going to just leave it alone; Alright, bro, so what do we need to get in this room for the little robot things," Justin replies to Jalen, acting weird.

"Okay, so I low-key got a little list for us, so we know exactly what we need to get; where's your phone?" he says to Justin about the materials for the project.

"My phone is right in my pocket; what's up?" he looks at Jae and asks him.

"Cool, this is what I want you to do with your phone; Take a picture of the list I got right here, and we basically split in half and get everything we need," he explains to him his plan.

"See, I'm better with pictures than I am with names of stuff," he then replies to him.

Jalen laughs and elucidates how the room is set up for Justin.

"Why did I know you would say something goofy like that? Everything in this room is actually organized by name to in alphabetical order as well, so it shouldn't be too hard to find stuff, actually. You think you got it, bro."

"Well, when you put it that way, it actually doesn't sound too hard, so, yeah, I'm sure I got it, nerd," he says, laughing.

Jalen looks over at Justin and chuckles, and throws him a lab coat for him to wear in the lab. Justin catches the jacket and puts it on. The two are both scavenging around the room for the equipment they need. After a couple of minutes, Jalen and Justin finish grabbing everything they need for the projects. They both walk out of the room, but before Jalen walks out of the room, he turns the lights off. The two start to walk down the hallway and go to Bernard's lab to build and design the robots.Bernard finishes his food from Roll up Rob's restaurant.

Bernard burps after taking a sip from the soda he had in the cup he was holding.

"Damn, Jae, your brother always knows how to throw down because those onion rings were so good. I needed that more than anything. Philly cheesesteak egg roll," he says to them about his other grandson's restaurant as they walk into the room. He throws his plate away in the trash can.

He starts laughing at his Grandfather says." I bet it was good because you ate the whole entire thing."

"Yeah, I didn't think you eat all the food he sent for you," Justin says to him after witnessing him eat all his food.

He starts laughing at both of them for what they said and says. "Yeah, I didn't think so either, but I couldn't help myself. I haven't had anything to eat since 630 this morning, so yeah, I really needed that, guys thank you."

Jalen walks over to his Grandfather to show him the list and says to him. "Okay, grandpa, we got everything off the list, so we should be good to start our experiments for the robots."

Bernard grabs his lab coat and starts to hold the materials out of the cart, and puts stuff on the tables. Jalen walks over to the 3d printer that his Grandfather has in the lab and turns it on. Justin walks over and grabs three pairs of safety goggles.

"Alright, boys, let's go ahead and get started. This is gonna be fun," he says to Justin and Jalen, all the designs. The 3 of them begin to start working on multiple designs. Justin stays on the computer to run diagnostics on the software for the robots. In contrast, Jalen runs back and forth to the 3d printer to get the materials to assemble the robots. Bernard starts putting the software chips into the mini-robots. Hours pass by, they finish 3 out of 4 designs, and Bernard is exhausted. Jalen fell asleep in a computer chair, and Justin fell asleep on the little futon in the lab.

Bernard wipes his eyes and yawns. He then looks over at Jalen and Justin sleeping and looks down at his watch. Bernard sees the time and realizes it's 1030.

Bernard then says to him." Oh damn, Jae and Justin, it's 1030; you all need to get home. It's late for a school night."

"Oh man, it's a good thing I told my parents I would come home late because I was helping y'all out," Justin says to Bernard after waking up.

"Alright, grandpa, let me go ahead and get Justin home before my mom gets me for coming home late," he says to his Grandfather Bernard as he and Justin start to pack their stuff up to leave and go home.

Bernard walks over to them, fist bumps them both, and says to them." Alright, boys, I will see you two later."

"Later, grandpa, I will call you and let you know I made it back home, and don't stay too late yourself, grandpa," he says to his grandpa as they begin to leave out the door.

"Peace out, grandpa. I will see you at the game later this week on Friday," Justin says to Bernard as he begins to follow Jalen out the door to leave out the building.

They get into the car and drive off down the street.

Bernard walks back to his lab and puts the cart of equipment back in the supply room; he looks down at the junk project box and pushes it to the back of the shelf. He then puts everything up and turns all the lights off in the room. He walks into his office and his lab and turns everything off for the night, and gathers his belonging to get ready and go home.

They arrive at Justin's house for him to get dropped off at home. Justin yawns and grabs his book bag, and exits the car.

He then walks over to Jalen's side of the car as he rolls down the window. He daps Jalen up and says to him." Catch you later. I'll see you at school in the morning."

Justin then walks up to his driveway to his front porch, unlocks his front door, and walks into the house.

Jalen then backs out of the driveway and begins to drive home. Time passes by, and Jalen arrives home. He parks his car, turns it off, and removes the keys from the ignition. He then gathers his belongings out of his car, walks to his front door, and quietly opens the door, so his mom doesn't hear him.

He then walks up the stairs tiptoeing to go to his room. Just before he gets to the stairs, his mom turns the light in the living room.

"Jalen, where have you been? It's 11 on a school night?" Lisa Collins asks him as she sits down in the chair.

"Okay, ma, don't be mad. I have a logical explanation for the time," he says to his mom, scared of possibly getting punished.

"Okay, I'm waiting; what is it," she then says to him, and she begins to get out of the chair to walk across the room to Jalen.

He tells his mom as he begins to take his phone out of his pocket to call his Grandfather. "Yeah, I'm definitely in the wrong for coming in this late. I should've told you I would be home a little later. I'm going to call grandpa real quick because that's where I was all this time. We got so caught up in this new experiment slash project we were working on, and I just came from Justin off."

The phone starts ringing as they sit there and wait for him to answer.

Bernard picks up the phone and says." Yo Jae, did you make it home, kid."

He puts the phone on speaker and tells his grandpa. "Yeah, grandpa, I just made it in and could tell my mom I was with you for the last 3 to 5 hours working on a new project."

"Yeah, mousey, he was with me; we really lost track of time. I'm sorry." Bernard says to his daughter about Jalen coming home so late.

"Thank you, grandpa I'm going to talk to you later, okay," Jalen replies to his Grandfather.

"Alright, Jae, I'll talk to you later, kid; love you guys good night," he then says on the phone to them, then hangs up.

"Don't come in here late again like that without calling me and letting me know you're going to be late," she says to her son about coming late.

Jalen walks over to his mom and says. "Okay, ma, I got you. I'm going to take a shower then get in the bed goof night ma love you," he then gives her a hug and a kiss on the cheek.

"Okay, see you in the morning, Jae, and love you too," she says to Jalen as he walks up the stairs to his room.

He walks up the stairs, peeks into his parents' room, and says. "What's up, dad? I'm about to go to sleep?"

"Yo, what's up, Jae," Rashawn says to Jalen as he walks past their room.

He walks into his room and tosses his book bag on the floor next to his bug. When it lands on the floor, the suit falls out slightly. Jalen walks to his bathroom and takes a shower. 30 minutes pass by, and Jalen comes out of the bathroom and gets ready for bed. He gets his phone charger out of his backpack. Jalen then sets up his phone to charge for the night. He then sets his alarm to get up for school in the morning. Right before he turns over and goes to sleep, he turns on his favorite cartoon show to watch and falls asleep too.

Chapter 3

At 550 on Wednesday morning, Jalen's alarm goes off for him to get up and get ready for school. He hit snooze on his alarm clock and went back to sleep for 5 minutes afterward. He gets up and goes into his bathroom to brush his teeth and wash his face. After being in the bathroom for a little Jalen goes back into his room across the hall. He yawns as he opens the door and walks around into his room.

Jalen opens his closet door and says."Damn, I really don't even know what to wear today. I should probably hurry up and find something before it gets too late. I still have to pick up the robot from grandpa."

Jalen keeps looking through his closet, and he picks out a thing of black sweatpants and a black graphic sweatshirt. He now sits on the floor and contemplates what sneakers he will wear for the day. Jalen ends up picking up a pair of red black sneakers.

His mom yells upstairs to Jalen and says."Jalen, are you up for school because it's almost 630."

Jalen yells back down and says."Yeah, I'm up, ma; I'm actually about to leave out right now."

Jalen begins to grab all his belongings to go downstairs and head out of the house. When he gets downstairs, his mom says to him. "Hey, I made a smoothie and some cinnamon rolls. Go ahead and start your car up so it can warm up. I will pack your cinnamon roll in a little container and smoothie in a cup."

Jalen looked into the kitchen sees and responded to her saying. "Okay, sounds cool. I will be right back."

Jalen grabs his belongings and walks out of the house to put them in the car. He sets his backpack in the passenger seat of his car. He then puts the key in the car's ignition and turns it on. He then goes inside to get his mom's cinnamon roll and smoothie. He grabs it from her and then hugs and kisses her cheek. Jalen walks back out the door, gets in his car, and drives off. Jalen begins to drive to his grandfather's office to pick up the robots.

"Damn, let me call grandpa and tell him I'm on the way there," he says to himself as he drives down the street.

Jalen calls his grandfather on the phone to tell him, and the phone starts ringing.

"Yeah, good morning Jae; what's up?" Grandpa says to him as he answers the phone.

"Hey, what's up, grandpa? I was actually coming to get the robots for the robotics club today," He says to his grandfather as he rides down the road.

"Okay, Jae, I got you. Just let me know when you get here, and I will bring them both out to the car," he says to his Grandson as he walks around his office, turning everything on in the facility while being on the phone.

He says to Bernard as he stops at a red light.

"Grandpa, I'm actually like five minutes away from you right now, so, if you want to, you could load them up. So by the time I get there, you'll be outside, and I could jet for school."

"Okay, sounds good, Jae. I'm actually standing right infant of them, so I'm going to load them up and roll them out right now," he says to Jae as he starts loading up the robots.

A few minutes pass by he arrives at Bernard's facility. Bernard comes outside with the robots loaded up on a cart. He gets out of the car to help his grandfather Bernard.

"Grandpa, do you think I should put them in the backseat or the trunk?" Jae Says to Bernard when he gets out of the car.

"Honestly, Jae, it depends on which one has more space," Bernard says to Jae, grabbing the cart.

The two of them try to get the robots into the car. Jalen puts 1 of the robots in the backseat and the other one in the trunk. He gets in the car and drives off from his grandfather's facility. Bernard waves at him as he begins to drive off. Bernard walks inside and locks the door.

He arrives at school, parks in his usual parking spot, and gets out. He locks his car doors and walks inside the school. Jalen walks down the hall to Mr. Martin's classroom to tell him about the robots for the fight later today. He gets to Mr. Martin's class, knocking on the door. He steps into the room and says. "What's up, Mr. Martin?"

"What's up, Jae? What are you doing here so early?" Mr.Martin asks him as he takes a sip of his coffee.

He says to Mr.Martin as he is standing in the classroom. "I was coming to tell you I got the robots for the fight later tonight. They're in my car right now. Before I actually brought them in, I just wanted to let you know."

Mr.Martin puts his coffee down and asks him. "Really, when are you going to bring them in? Can I see a picture of them too?"

Jalen walks over to Mr. Martin's desk and tells him, "I'm going to bring it in later during the sixth period if that's fine with you. I don't have any pictures of them, my bad."

Mr.Martin slides back from his desk, closes his laptop, and says to Jalen."That's fine because we're going to have a meeting anyway before the fight."

"Okay, sounds cool! If I'm late to class, I'm getting them out of the car," he says to Mr.Martin as he begins to walk out of the room.

The day goes by, and it's lunchtime. Jalen eats his lunch as he sits at the table with Justin, Maya, and Brea.

"Are you guys coming to the robotics club thing tonight?" Jalen asks them before he finishes his slice of pizza.

"Hell no, bro, you know I'm not coming to the nerd thing," says Justin as he looks up from his phone.

"Damn, that's crazy because you helped create the two robots, so you're actually a nerd," he then implies to Justin as he holds the pizza crust.

Justin smirks at him and goes back to looking down at his phone.

Maya taps Jalen's arm as she sits next to him and asks. "If you need someone there to support you, I could come, Jae."

The two of them look each other in the eyes, and Jalen says to her. "Yeah, it would really mean a lot if you came. That's only if you want to come through."

"Jae, I mean, yeah, I will let you know right after the sixth period if I'm coming," Maya says to him as she contemplates if she's going.

The school bell rings for the next period, so kids in the cafeteria get up and walk in the hallway to get to their next class for the day. Jalen gets up from the table and walks to his car to get the robots. He gets to his car and now wonders how he will bring them in by himself.

Jalen thinks of a plan for Justin to come outside to help him real quick, so he texts Justin real quick to see. Justin receives the text and says to Mr. Martin,

"Mr.Martin Jalen actually needs help with the robots and is wondering if I could come out and help him real quick."

Mr.Martin looks up from his computer, looks over at Justin, and says. "Yeah, that's fine, but don't take too long."

Justin gets up, leaves his backpack, and walks out of the classroom with just his phone on his body. Justin walks out of the school to meet Jalen at his car to get the robots.

Justin starts walking up to Jalen.

Jalen says to him. "Aye, bro, these things are heavy, but they're small. We can each carry one."

Justin looks inside Jalen's car and tells him. "They don't really look all that heavy."

Jalen picks up one of the robots and responds to him."Dude, shut up and pick up the other one."He picks up the other one and says. "Actually, you know what? This thing is low-key heavy."

The two of them begin to walk back to the classroom and struggle on the way because the robots are heavy, so they have to stop a couple of times. After like ten minutes, they finally got inside the classroom. The two of them show up to class out of breath.

Mr.Martin walks over to them, grabs the robots, and asks. "Are you guys okay?"

Jalen walks over to his desk and says." Yeah, it was just a long walk, and I was ready to sit down."

Some time passes by, and it's the end of the day. The robotics club is getting ready for its fight. 7 different schools are set to come to Northview High School. Before the matches start, the Northview High robotics club must decide what robot to use. Mr. Martin and Jalen show the robots to the rest of the students to vote. The first one is an all-black two-and-a-half-foot tall robot with an 8-inch battering ram in the front in the shape of a ram's head with a reinforced metal of 3 layers behind the ram head. Shoots fire out the ram's mouth. The second robot is effortless but has a more solid body design with a metal frame to withstand blows from other robots.

The robotics club chooses the first design to fight tonight's matches.

Jalen inputs a computer chip into the first robot design to activate the team's controls. The Northview club consists of Mr. Martin as the coach, and Jalen is the team captain. Andrew Hayward is the co-captain and main attacker. Olivia Scott and Jeremy James and movement control. The four of them breeze through the first two matches with no problem. Jalen notices that

Maya sits there behind him before the last game starts.

Jalen smiles and waves at Maya and says. "I honestly didn't think you were coming. I thought it would be a little boring to you." He starts laughing at Maya.

Maya looks at Jalen, laughs at what he says, and replies to him. "Yeah, I mean, it's very different from what I expected. I'm actually enjoying myself, though."

Jalen smiles at Maya; he then turns around and gathers with his team before the night's last match to go over strategy. The club came up with a plan as they watched their opponents throughout the night.

Mr.Martin sits down, looks at the team, and asks them. "Have you guys seen a weak point in those Maple creek kids' robots?"

Jalen looks over at Andrew and sees what he has.

Andrew looks up from his tablet and says to Mr. Martin. "Yeah, I think it's a weakness on the middle of both sides because it's not protected there. I've been analyzing that spot each one of their fights."

Jalen looks over at the robot, analyzes it with his eyes, and starts thinking of multiple strategies to counter and attack their armor by surprise.

Jalen says to the team. "Okay, guys, I have a plan. Just trust me on this. I think we can do this. Our bot is much faster. They're a defensive team like us, so if we punk them into attacking first by faking like we will attack. We can counter that and smash their side."

Mr.Martin looks over at the opponent's bot, looks back at the team, and says. "Yeah, I think that could work, Jae. What do you think, guys?"

Andrew, Olivia, and Jeremy all nod their head agreeing with the plan in hopes that it could work. They all put their hands together and come out of their team circle, ready to execute the goal to win.

Maya stands up behind them in the crowd and Screams out of excitement. "Let's go, Northview; you got this!"

Jalen turns around, looks at her, and smiles.

Jalen and Mr. Martin place the bot within the ring, ready for the official to call for the start of the match. Their opponents on maple creek look over, trying to intimidate them before the game. The official looks at both teams and rings the bell. The robots roll towards each other. Jalen signals to the team down attack yet, basically saying remember our strategy. Maple creek circles around Northview bot planning to finally make their move. Just as soon as Maple Creek tries to attack, Northview counters it with a full-speed ram into the side of the Maple Creek bot. The robot starts to spin out of control from the hit for a couple seconds into the barrier.

Jalen signals his team forward and says. "Now that's it full speed, one more hit."

Northview rams Maple Creek one more time but with more force than the first time, causing the back wheels to fall. The robot struggles to move around. Northview plans another attack to win, and they ram it again. The hit demobilizes the robot. Northview wins their first bot tournament ever in school history. They get presented this big trophy with a robot on it. Maya looks over at them, being the one clapping for them and cheering on them.

Andrew looks at Jalen, fist bumps him, and says. "Good call Jae with that plan to attack and be patient."

Jalen fist bumps him back and says. "This victory is all you, dude; you're the one that found their weakness, not me, so take credit for this win; you deserve it."

Mr. Marin says to all of the team. "I'm really proud of you kids working together and pulling through. That's what it's all about when you're on a team."

Some minutes pass by, and everyone starts to leave the match. All the members are gathering there belongs to leave and go home. Jalen walks out of the robot fighting arena and right out the door. He sees Maya standing right there waiting for him.

Jalen looks up in shock that she waited for him and says." What's up, Maya? I'm surprised you are still here."

"I mean, yeah, Brea dropped me off real quick, and I just needed a ride back home; that's why I'm waiting for you, Jae," she says to him as they start walking out of the arena together smiling and laughing.

He looks over at her and implies. "You already know I got you." Jalen pulls his keys out of his backpack to unlock his car.

Maya laughs and says. "Jae, but I still thought it should ask you because you could have something to do."

They walk up to his car, and he unlocks his car. Opens the door for her and says. "Maya, you know damn well it doesn't bother me."

She gets in the car after.

Jalen gets in the car and throws his backpack in the backseat. The two of them rode down the road to her house. Time passes by the two of them finally arrive at her home.

Jae gets out of the car and opens her door to help her out of his car. He then walks her to her front door.

He then grabs her hand before she walks into the house, hugs her, and tells her. "Thanks for coming; it really meant a lot."

"Yeah, no problem, it actually really liked it," she says to him as she looks up at him. The two of them begin to gaze into each other eyes and start moving closer as if they were going to kiss.

Maya's mom opens the door, and the two of them begin to act awkward because they almost kiss.

Maya's mom steps outside and says."Hey Jalen, how have you been?" She then opens her arms to give him a hug.

He then gives her mom a hug and says."Hey, I'm doing pretty well; Mrs. Wilson, what about yourself."

Mrs. Wilson looks over at Maya and says."I'm doing good. I just actually finished dinner; if you would like to stay."

Maya looks over at him, giving him a look like she is saying no.

He looks over at Mrs. Wilson and says. "No, I actually have to get home right about now."

Mrs. Wilson looks at him and says." Well, maybe next time if you're in the area."

He gives Maya a side hug bye because of the awkward moment and walks to his to get in his car, and begins to drive away.

Maya and her mom walk inside the house. Maya takes her things to her room and Calls Brea.

"Brea, I got to tell you what almost happened," Maya immediately says to Brea as she answers the phone.

"Damn, hold on, what happened with you two?" Brea says to Maya, kind of caught off guard with the fast approach.

Maya laughs on the phone and says. "We actually almost kissed tonight."

Brea jumps up in her bed in surprise at what Maya said to her and responds back with. "Wait, what? How did you guys even get that close?"

Maya shrugs her shoulder and says to Brea. "I don't even know; we just hugged again and had an adorable moment. Right when it was about to happen, my mom came out.""Damn, really, that sucks for real," she said to Maya.Maya laughs and says to her.

"Yeah, I know; let me call you back. I'm actually about to go eat dinner real quick."

"Alright, sounds cool; just call me later," Brea says to Maya right before the phone hangs up on her.

Maya gets up from her bed. She Goes downstairs, washes her hand, and decides to make herself a plate of food.

Time passes by. Jalen is at home, just finished dinner, and is relaxing in the room when he looks over and sees the suit he took from his grandfather's lab. Jalen jumps up from his bed and picks the suit up. He looks at the suit and decides to try it on. He puts it on and seems baggy, then the suit self-adjusts itself to fit Jalen's body.

He walks over to his mirror and starts posing in the bodysuit. He starts to throw punches to see how flexible the suit is. He looks down and sees a little thing of his vitals on his wristband and starts to look really confused by that. He decides to take it off and puts it down where it was before.

He then actually chooses to lay down and get ready for bed. He doesn't know that the suit just sent out a homing beacon to a Mysterious person.

A mysterious man sits down in a chair, realizing he just got the location of the bodysuit. He gets up, starts walking around his secret base, and begins to mobilize his plans to get to that location of the suit with his small militia. He prints out the state location of where the bodysuit is.

"I'm coming for you, Bernard," The mystery man says aloud to himself as he looks at the coordinates of the suit being identified.

1 day passes by; it's Friday, and Northview high school is getting ready for the big rivalry basketball game versus Maple Creek. The doors to the gymnasium are opening up for the game to start. Brea, Maya, and Justin all walk into the gym and walk to the best seats they can find in the student section to watch for the varsity.

Justin says to Maya as the student section starts to get loud.

"You know Maya, I'm actually stunned you came because I know you hate many loud noises. Trust me, it's really about to be loud in here."

"I don't think it will be that bad," Maya says to Justin, looking around in the student section.

"You do realize this game is our rivalry game, right?" Brea asks Maya as she looks at her, confused.

Coach Walters is in the varsity basketball locker room, looking at his playbook. Jalen has his headphones listening to his music to get himself in game mode.

Coach Walters walks up to him and asks. "Did you ever go over that play I gave you?"

He looks up at Coach and says. "Yeah, I went over five times to make sure I have it down and memorized."

Coach fist bumps him and says. "Okay, good, just in case it's a close game and it comes down to that play, I need you to make the right decision when the time comes."

He looks back at Coach and says. "You know I got you, Coach, don't worry."

He puts his headphones on, continues to listen to his music, closes his eyes, and takes a deep breath to focus and tune out all the noise around him.

Back out in the gymnasium, Maya gets up and goes to the concession stand to get some chips and a drink. She sees Jalen's mom and grandpa and goes over to them and says. "Hey, Ms. Lisa and Grandpa, how are you guys?"

Lisa Collins looks over and hugs Maya as soon as she sees her and says. "Hey boo, how are you?"

Grandpa looks and hugs Maya and says. "Hey Maya, how have you been?"

Maya smiles at both of them and says. "I've been pretty good, to be honest. Jae persuaded me to come to the game tonight; that's the only reason why I'm here."

Lisa looked at her, smiled, and said to her. "I don't understand why he doesn't just make a move already."

She looks at Lisa, surprised at what she says. "What do you mean, Ms. Lisa?"

She then responds to her and simply says, expressing how she feels about them. "I see Jalen's face and how he acts whenever your name is mentioned. As his mom, I probably shouldn't say this, but everyone knows you like him, and he likes you too."

Maya smiled back at Ms. Lisa and said. "Dang, is it really that obvious that everyone can see it? I'm just waiting for him to make the first move."

Bernard looks at Maya and says. "Just be straightforward and tell him tonight. I'm pretty sure you two will hang out after the game."

Maya looks at grandpa and laughs.

Lisa says to Maya. "No, honestly, that's what you should do. You can't wait for him to make the first move so go ahead."

Maya laughs and smiles at both of them and says. "Yeah, I will; thanks, you guys."

Maya begins to walk away to sit back down with Justin and Brea. The varsity game starts soon; the teams finally come out on the floor and begin to do the normal pregame shoot-around and warmups.

Jalen comes out looking super focused yet relaxed at the same time. The team warms up for about fifteen minutes or so.

Northview and Maple Creek go to the benches to introduce the starters for the night. The first announces all the Maple Creek starters because they are the visiting team. They then turn out the lights, and a spotlight comes on Northview to introduce their starting lineup.

Right before Jalen gets his name called, he takes a deep breath and tunes out all of the crowd's noise to remain focused. They call his name, and he gets up and runs onto the floor with his teammates. He fist bumps all the officials reffing the game and fists bumps the Maple Creek team and coaching staff. The two teams starting five get ready at center court for the jump ball to start the game. The referee gets the game ball walks to the center court, blows his whistle, and throws the ball up for the jump ball, signaling the start of the game. The crowd is super loud in both student sections. Both student sections start stomping on the bleachers making noise, ready for the game.

A couple quarters pass by; it's now the fourth quarter with two minutes left in the game, and Northview is down by 7. Coach Walters is sweating, looking down in his playbook.

He calls a timeout, brings his team into the huddle, and says. "Okay, guys, this is our court; let's go out there and make some good defensive stops. We need a couple of good-looking shots to tie this thing or take the lead. Jalen, I want you to focus on getting the ball in the paint for two possessions. The interior defense is weak. Focus on defending the three-ball as well; that's their strength. Let's go out there and win us a game."

The buzzer sounds indicate the timeout is over. Northview walks back to the courts. Northview inbounds the ball, and Jalen brings the ball up the court. He comes across half-court, and his teammate sets a pick for him; Jalen dribbles up to the three-point line and shoots a jumper, and it goes in. Everyone in the Northview section starts yelling with excitement. He looks up at Maya and winks. Maya then smiles back at him. He turns around and jogs to get back on defense and the rest of his teammates on the court.

He then looks up at the scoreboard and sees that it a one minute and forty-seconds left in the game, and he screams out to his teammates and says. "Lock up and stay on your man like glue."

Maple Creek inbounds the ball and begins to bring it up the court, setting up their offense. Jalen's teammates start to play really intense defense on their matchups. The point guard comes across half-court, dribbles up to the three-point line, and passes the ball into the paint, and it gets deflected. Northview comes up with the steal with a minute and twenty-five seconds left down 4 points with the 67 Maple Creek 63 Northview. Northview runs down the court.Jalen calls for the ball, stands there for a second, and signals his team to calm down. He points at the scoreboard to let his team know we have more than enough time on the board, so stay focused. Jalen dribbles down the court and dribbles to the left of the three-point line. The Center on Northview comes up to the man guarding Jalen and sets a pick on him. The center does a pick and roll; he then cuts to the basket. Jalen passes the ball to him, and he gets fouled. He goes to the foul line to shoot free throws. The center shakes his head because he's not a good free-throw shooter.

Jalen walks up to him and tells him. "Isaiah, we only need one; just remember that and focus."

Isaiah gets the ball to shoot the first two free throws. He takes three dribbles, spins the ball in his left hand, and shoots the ball with his left hand. The ball swirls around the rim and falls out. He misses and looks down in disappointment.

Jalen looks over at him and says. "Take your time and focus; you got this, bro."

Isaiah takes a deep breath, does his free throw routine again, and hits the backboard. The ball kisses the backboard and goes right in. Maple Creek inbounds the ball brings it up the court and starts to pass it around for fifteen-seconds above the three-point line before. The score is now 67-64, with five-seconds left in the game.

Coach Walters looks at them, looks at the clock, and notices they are wasting time. Coach Walters throws his clipboard and screams out. "Foul them they're trying to run the clock!"

With forty-seconds left, Jalen fouls one of the Maple creek players down three points. They don't go to the free-throw line because they're not over the limit yet. Maple creek inbounds the ball, and it gets stolen as he runs by; he slows down the game's tempo and waits for all his teammates to bring it down the court. He waits for the offense set up and passes to his teammate on the wing; he shoots a three and makes it with Twenty-three seconds left. Jalen then screams to his team. "Get back on defense, now let's go!" The game is now tied 67-67. Maple Creek gets the ball in and brings it up; they start passing it around and try to score inside the paint. They get fouled and miss the shot attempt.

Maple Creek goes to free throw for two. Northview's student section starts booing the Maple Creek player at the free throw.

Justin stands up and yells out." Yeah, boo, you're going to miss!" Trying to disrupt Maple Creek's focus in the game.

Maple player misses both free and Northview student section cheers. Northview rebounds the ball after the second miss. Coach Walters calls a timeout and looks at the clock sees 9 seconds left with the game tied at 67.Coach Walters brings his team into the huddle, telling Jalen."It's time for that play; remember, you have two choices in the play. You can shoot the jumper or drive whichever one is open at the time; take it, don't hesitate."

Jalen looks at Coach as he sips some water from his water bottle and says. "Okay, coach, I'm ready."

Coach brings his hand in, and everybody puts their hand on top of his, and he says, "Let's go win a game! Rams, let's go on three. 1! 2! 3!"

They all scream Rams ending the huddle. The crowd begins to yell repeatedly. " Let's go, Rams."

Northview inbounds the ball, and Isaiah gets the ball; he passes it to Jalen. Jalen moves to the right of the three-point line and waits for a teammate to set a pick. He dribbles away from his defender and shoots the fadeaway jumper; twenty feet away, it goes off in the glass, bank shots in, and the buzzer sounds. This indicates the end of the game, with 69-67 Northview wins.

He falls down after his fadeaway shot and gets up immediately after the shot. Everyone in the Northview section starts cheering so loud. Maya, Brea, and Justin are cheering because Jalen hit the game-winner. The two teams line up and shake hands to show good sportsmanship. Some students walk on the court to celebrate the victory with the team against their school rival. After the game, the school plans to celebrate at Let's roll up Rob's restaurant. After the game, Jalen and the rest of his team come out of the locker room fully dressed in their street clothes. They All get ready to leave the gym to go celebrate the win.

Everybody gets to the restaurant, and it's packed inside and outside. The students ordered cinnamon roll egg rolls and apple pie egg rolls with hot chocolate and other food items. Jalen finally gets to the restaurant and parks his car, goes inside to see rob and looks for his friends. He orders some food from rob and some hot chocolate and goes outside. Maya, Brea, and Justin all sit outside laughing and drinking hot chocolate when he finally walks up to them.

"Jae, what's up, Mr big shot," Justin says to him as he fist bumps him.

Brea takes a sip of her hot chocolate and says. "Yeah, Jae, I'm not going to lie; it was a nice shot."

"Yeah, it was all because the coach drew up this play earlier in the week. He knew it would be a good game and thought it could come down to the wire." He laughs, shrugs his shoulders, and says.

"Yeah, you could ask them both; I was cheering super loud after you hit that shot," Maya says to him, and she sips her hot chocolate.

He looks over at Maya, smiles, and says. "Damn, really, I couldn't even imagine you screaming at any sporting event."

Justin drinks his hot chocolate and eats his apple pie egg roll. He then says. "Bro, what she was yelling louder than I've ever heard your mom cheer, dude."

Maya looks away from Jalen, sips her hot chocolate in embarrassment, and laughs.

Justin and Brea look at each other and decide to get up.

"Hey Justin, can you come with me to get some egg rolls? I'm kind of hungry now," Brea says to him as the two of them leave to give Jalen and Maya some space to talk.

Justin looks at Jalen and winks at him. Brea walks over to Maya, whispers into her ear, and says. "This is the time to make your move on him, hopefully. If he doesn't make a move, please just tell him how you feel." Brea and Justin begin to walk away.

Jalen sits down next to Maya at an outside table, and the two share an awkward moment of silence. He looks over at Maya and says. "what are your plans for the winter break since you will be home the whole holiday?"

Maya looks up and says to him. "Honestly, I'm really not doing anything but some Christmas shopping tomorrow or Sunday; that's about it, Jae."

He looks at her, smiles, and says. "Yeah, I feel you. I'm trying to figure out what to do myself. Wait, we could do some Christmas shopping together on Sunday if you want to."

"Wait, you would really want to do that together," Maya smiles and says to him as they sit and enjoy their hot cocoa together.

He says to her. "Maya, we've been friends forever since elementary school, but I want to be more than friends. I've had the biggest crush on you for a while."

She smiles and grabs his arm, and says to him. "Jalen, I've actually had a crush on you since seventh grade. I haven't known how to tell you. I was scared you wouldn't think of the same."

The two of them smiled at each other and hugged each other. Maya then kisses him on the cheek, grabs his arm, and leans on him. The two of them sit there laughing and talking, waiting for Justin and Brea to return. A couple of minutes passed by, and Justin and brea came back and sat down, and they all started talking. The four of them begin to enjoy themselves for another hour and a half, having fun amongst everyone there at Let's roll-up. They all get up to leave the restaurant. He drops Justin off at home so Justin can finish packing to go out of town with his family. Brea then drops Maya off at home to go home and get for her family trip. He gets home and starts texting Maya about their plans for tomorrow.

Chapter 4

Two high-tech cargo planes arrive at a private airfield in Georgia, hiding on the radar the next day. The two cargo planes land on the airstrip and unload their stuff onto trucks inside a hangar. When four cop cars and Security of the airfield show up at the hangar. One of the cops takes cover behind the police cruiser and says. "Okay, hands up and get on the ground." All the cops get out of the car with their weapons drawn immediately.

The mysterious man wearing a hoodie says. "Tyler can go handle that for me; they're in my way." Tyler looks at the mysterious man; the second in command looks over at him and smiles. Tyler then starts walking to them slowly. One of the cops, with his weapon drawn, says. "Don't come any closer, or we will shoot."

Tyler then draws the two swords on his back and charges at the cops. The cops start shooting at him, and he runs side-to-side, dodging the bullets. He then swipes his swords at the police officers' weapons, stabbing and slicing through them.

He then stands over their bodies and says. "That was actually kind of fun. I haven't had any action in a while." He walks back over to the cargo planes to unload their equipment.

The mysterious man says to Tyler. "We've got a lot of work to do now." He then smiles, looking around at his militia. He walks over to one of the trucks and goes and sits inside, waiting for them to finish.

Tyler takes over as the rest of the militia still unload the planes with everything. He then goes over a checklist of everything needed to be loaded up. The militia begins to set explosive charges around the hangar. Tyler drags all the cops' bodies out of the hangar onto grass 50 to 100 feet. 30 minutes passed by, and the group of men finally finished loading the truck with the stuff they needed. Tyler then locks down the planes and closes the bay doors of them. He then walks over to his boss is sitting in the truck. He knocks on the window. The mysterious man rolls down the window and says. "What is it? Have they finished loading up the equipment?"

Tyler says to his boss."Yeah, they just finished, and I went over the checklist to ensure we got everything off. The charges are set around the hangar as well."

"Alright, get in the truck; we're leaving from here right now. Go tell the wheels up now," The mysterious man says to Tyler Shaw.

The mysterious man sits and looks over at Tyler in the driver's seat and tells him. "Go ahead and do it now." The rest of the men load up their personal belongings into the trucks and get in, and they leave the airfield.

Tyler looks back at him and says. "Wait, do what, boss? You know you gotta be more specific with me."

The mysterious man then looks back and says. "Detonate the explosive, you damn idiot."

Tyler chuckles at his boss and says. "Oh yeah, I mean, I knew that."

Tyler looks down at the remote device and detonates all the explosives planted in the hangar. The aircraft hangar blows up and falls down from all the explosives. They begin to start driving away from the airfield. When all emergency departments go in the fire's direction to see if anyone was hurt. The anonymous man and his militia entirely flee the scene. They start to drive to their planned hideout. To set up all of the equipment for a base of operations.

Jalen wakes up on Sunday excited for the day because he gets to hang out with Maya and spend the entire day with her. He gets up and goes brushes his teeth, and washes his face. Once he finishes, he goes downstairs to make himself something to eat to get his day started. He turns on the television to watch some morning cartoons. When he turns it on, it's on the news about an explosion and cops dead at a private airfield. Jalen shakes his head in disbelief.

He then turns to some cartoons and sits with his bowl of cereal at the table.

Lisa Collins comes downstairs and says. "What's up, baby? What do you have planned for the day?"

He looks over at his mom and says. "What's up, ma? Maya and I will go hang out and do Christmas shopping together today."

Lisa smiled and picked up her cup of coffee and took a sip. She then says. "It's about time y'all finally hang out together and spend some time with each other."

He laughs and says, "Don't tell you knew the whole time she liked me and never said anything either."

Lisa chuckles and says back to him. "Yes, why do you think I always say she is such a sweet girl and that y'all would be cute together."

Jalen then tells his mom. "All this time, everyone has known we liked each other except for us. Now I feel dumb because all of the clues have been right in my face."

"I actually told her the other night at the game that she should just make the first move; she said she's been waiting for you to make a move this whole time," Lisa says to him as he starts looking confused.

He starts laughing at his mom and looks super confused, and says. "Wait, you guys spoke the other night at the game."

Lisa nodded her head and said. "Yeah, and grandpa was telling her to do the same thing because we all love her, and she is basically already a part of the family."

He looks shocked and says. "Dang, grandpa was saying that too. Justin has been telling me for a while. He said to hang out with her on the winter break to spend quality time with her. He and Brea are going out of town."

Lisa sipped her coffee and said to him. "Honestly, that is true; this is the perfect time for you and her to hang out. Go ice skating with her, or do gingerbread house making, which would be fun. You could bring her over, and y'all could watch Christmas movies and drink hot chocolate."

He looks up and laughs at her and says. "Okay, ma, I will watch more of my cartoons. I'm going to start getting ready in a little bit to hang out with her."

Lisa walked away and started to walk back upstairs with her coffee.

One hour and 15 minutes pass by, and Jalen is still watching TV. His tv show goes off, and he gets up and goes upstairs to his room. He then walks around his, planning his outfit for the day with Maya. He picks out what he wants to wear. He then grabs his underclothes, goes into his bathroom, and takes a shower for 20 mins.

Jalen walks out of the bathroom and goes into his bedroom with his underclothes and towel on his shoulders. He walks around his room and does stretching in it. He then looks down at the bodysuit and tries it on again. The suit's body vitals icon pops up on Jalen's wrist. He then grabs the phone and answers it. He notices that those vitals are his own, and he then gets a call from Maya.

Jalen looks and smiles at Maya as soon as he sees her face on the phone. Maya smiles back and says. "Hey Jae, what's up?"

"At the current moment, I'm actually getting ready," Jalen says to her on the phone.

She looks at him and laughs at him, and says. "Jae, you remember you were supposed to pick me up now."

"Ah damn, Maya, I'm so sorry I really lost track of time. I will definitely be there soon for real, I promise." He drops his jaw in shock at what Maya just said to him.

Maya smirks at him and says. "Okay, I believe you. Just hurry because I was really looking forward to spending most of the day with you. I'll see you in a little bit." She then hangs up the phone.He starts rushing to get dressed and then realizes he left the suit on under his clothes. He then grabs his car keys and runs out the front door. Jalen gets in his car and turns it on to warm it up. He turns on the heat in his car.

Jalen sets up his music in his car and drives to Maya's house. He then says out loud to himself. "Okay, while I'm waiting for the car to get warm, let me text Maya and let her know I'm leaving."

The anonymous man sits in his secret base with his militia. When a location of the suit pops up on the computers for them. The Anonymous man looks at his militia and tells them. "Go retrieve the suit, and it will lead us to the serums to execute our plan."

Tyler shaw is leading the team on the pursuit. Tyler takes a group of 5 men with him. They all get into a truck and leave out the hideout.

Some time passes by, and he finally arrives at Maya's house. Jalen gets out of his car, walks to her front door, and rings the doorbell. Maya then comes to the door and opens it. She smiles and says. "Took you long enough, Jae."

Jalen smiles back at her and says. "My bad, I just really wasn't paying attention to the time, unfortunately."

She then hugs Jalen and says. "Jalen, it's okay. I'm not mad. Let me go get my coat, and we could go leave out." She then grabs her coat and walks out her front door. He and Maya walk off her front porch and walk to his car. He walks around and opens the door for her to get in the car, then he gets in the car. The two of them begin to leave and head to the mall.

Some time passes by Jalen and Maya walk around and go from store to store at the mall. The two of them look around and do some of their Christmas shopping. He grabs her hand as they're walking and the two start holding hands. She looks at him, starts smiling, and kisses him.

He smiliest at her and asks her. "Hey, you want to do something goofy as hell?"

Maya looks at him and says. "What'd you have in mind."

"I think it's something fun we could do; What if we went to take pictures with Santa?" He says to Maya.

She laughs at him and says. "Like, are you talking about sitting on the mall Santa's lap?"

He laughs at her and says. "No, I'm talking about taking goofy pictures with the mall Santa; How do you feel about that?"

Maya looks at him and says. "Yeah, we could; that actually sounds funny, not going to lie."

They both walk up to the mall Santa. The two of them walk to the mall Santa's location and get in line. After a couple of mins, the two of them are next in line.

They look at each other and start laughing. Jalen says to the mall Santa. "We just want to take goofy pictures with you if that's okay."

The mall Santa looks at them both and laughs, and says. "Yeah, come on, I'd love to."

They both stand on the sides of the Santa. The three of them sit there and pose, being funny and having a good time. The two of them start doing goofy poses, and the mall Santa begins to join in.

Afterward, Jalen and Maya get the photos they took with Santa. They stand there laughing at how goofy the pictures are, and the two start to walk around the mall a little more. The two ride the miniature train in the mall for kids being goofy. When they get done on the train ride around the mall, they start walking around, searching for something else to do. Jalen goes into a couple of sneaker stores and tries on some shoes that he likes. He then says to her. "You should try some things on; we didn't come to the mall just to buy everybody else stuff."

Maya smiles and says, "Okay, I'm gonna go look at some things that I like for me, okay."

They start going from store to store, trying on clothes and shoes. Neither one found anything they liked, so they didn't buy anything.

He then grabs Maya's hand and asks her. "Hey, would you want to get some hot chocolate together?"

She continues to look at the pictures they took and says. "Yeah, that actually sounds pretty good, Jae."

The two of them walk to one of the coffee shops in the mall to get some hot chocolate.

Tyler shaw tracks the suit's location to the mall that Jalen is at. Tyler and his men walk around the mall, trying to locate the person with the suit. Tyler searches for a couple of minutes and walks into a coffee shop, and the suit starts popping up on the radar.

Jalen and Maya stand in the coffee shop online, waiting to order their hot chocolates.

Tyler stands in the line in the coffee shop and sees Jalen, looks at him, and says. "Give me the suit right now and hand the serums over."

He turns around and says. "Dude, what are you talking about."

Maya looks over at Jalen, then looks at Tyler and says. "We don't know you, weirdo, so leave us alone."

Tyler steps in between Jalen and Maya and grabs Jalen, and says. "I know you have the suit on right now, but where are the serums?"

"Dude, I don't know what you are talking about; leave me alone," he says to Tyler as he pushes him away.

Tyler retaliates with a punch, and Jalen ducks. He grabs Maya, and they run out of the coffee shop. When they exit the coffee shop, Tyler shaw's team is outside waiting for Jalen. Jalen pushes one as he tries to run away, holding Maya's hand.

Shaw's team tries to corner Jalen. He then tells Maya, "Maya get out of here. I got this. Run, I will catch up with you, I promise."

She begins to start running from them.

One of Shaw's men tries to go after Maya, but Jalen throws some food at him and says. "Over here, tough guy, your fight is with me, come on."

Jalen starts fighting with Tyler's team, throws hot chocolate at the 2 of them, and hits one in the face with a food tray. People in the mall start screaming and running in panic. Jalen starts running away from them.

Tyler says to his team. "Come on, get him. We need to capture him." Tyler begins to chase after him on foot in the mall. Jalen starts running around the mall, jumping over things and dodging things as he runs. Shaw chases after Jae pushing people out the way and trying to stay close to Jae. As shaw and his team start chasing after Jalen. Weapons begin to form around their wrist out of thin air shooting tranquil darts.

Jalen turns around as he runs from them and says. "Wait, that's nanotech; what the heck."

Jalen starts to see darts fly toward him as he runs away. He then sees patterns and different angles to jump to and maneuver towards that help him escape. Jalen jumps in between two people, and Shaw ends up firing at him and missing and hitting a couple of civilians and knocking them out. He then jumps and falls to a lower level of the mall and continuously runs, trying to escape the men following him. He then grabs his phone out of his pocket as he's running and calls Maya on the phone.

Maya picks up the phone, and Jalen says. "Maya, listen, I need you to meet me at my car now."

"Okay, I'm on my way to it right now," Maya says to him as she begins running to the car.

Jalen continues running and says to Maya. "I will be there in a couple of minutes."

He hangs up the phone and tries to make a run for his car. Jalen loses Shaw and his team in a big mix of people walking in the mall.

Jae runs to the car and tells Maya. "Get in now; we have to go." The two of them get in the car and drive out of the mall parking lot.

Maya looks over at Jalen in the car and says. "Who were they, Jae?"

He continues driving down the road and says to her. "I don't know who they were."

"Why did they ask about a suit?" she then asks him. She sits there curious about everything that just happened in the mall.

He looks over at her for a quick second and says. "Look, Maya, I don't know what just happened. All I know is that I'm taking you home."

She says to him. "Wait, for what? We need to go to the police."

He replies to her saying. "Yeah, we will; we can talk about it later, but I need to see my grandfather, so you're going home, okay."

A couple of minutes pass by, they arrive at Maya's house, and he drops her off. Jalen rolls his window down and says to her. "I will call later tonight."

He then backs out of her driveway, and she walks inside the house. He then drives down the road for a while and goes to his Grandfather's office. He gets out of his car and buzzes the door for Bernard to open. The door opens, and Jalen goes straight to Bernard's office room.

Jalen walks in, sits down, and says to Bernard, "Grandpa, I have to tell you something."

Bernard looks over at Jalen and says. "Okay, what's up, Jae?"

Jalen exhales and says to Bernard. "Grandpa, I took that suit from your supplies closet."

Bernard drops his papers onto his desk and asks him. "What suit are you talking about?"

He lifts his shirt up and shows his Grandfather the suit under his clothes and then says. "This suit, grandpa, I'm sorry."

Bernard immediately runs over to him and says. "Take that off right now; they're tracking it. You have no idea what you've just done."

He starts trying to take the suit off and says. "Wait, who's tracking us, grandpa?"

Bernard helps him get the suit off and then asks."Were you followed here?"

Jalen looks at his Grandfather, confused at what's going on, and says to him. "I don't know. I don't think so."

Bernard grabs him and looks him dead in his eyes, and says. "Kid, I need you to be sure right now that you weren't followed. The person tracking this suit is dangerous."

He looks at Bernard and says. "Grandpa, I just got attacked in the mall with Maya. The people that attacked me were asking about the suit and something about some serums.

"He says to his grandson, "Damn, he's finally making his move on the serums."

"Grandpa, what are you talking about? Who finally making their move? What are these serums?" He begins asking Bernard because he's confused about what's going on.

Bernard sits down and tells him. "Jalen, I need you to listen to me very carefully, so take a seat."

He looks at Bernard with no idea what to say and sits down across from him. Bernard looks at Jalen with a face of frustration and takes a deep breath.

Bernard then says to him. "This all started in 1990. I was working on a secret project for the government. I worked for a company called GenXtech, where we did research on the human genome."

He then says to his Grandfather. "Wait for grandpa; I thought you were a regular scientist, not some type of government scientist."

He says back to him. "Unfortunately, I was not. I saw many things, many things from when I worked for them. There was an extraterrestrial that crashed down to earth around that time. We ran so many tests on the being, and his DNA was very close to human DNA. We then started making his blood into serums. The United States government wanted every other country to fear them. We made the serums for the soldiers to become super-soldiers."

He then says to him. "What the hell? That's crazy; this is insane."

Bernard looks at him and says. "You can't tell anyone about this. Do you understand me?" He then nods his head, replying to Bernard.

Bernard says to him. "While we were still testing the serums, my partner went through something very traumatic. The man lost his little brother due to police brutality, and he was never the same after that. Zion became a man full of rage and wanted to steal the serums from the government and sell it to gangs in the streets and the black market dealers to cripple the United States. This man wanted to strip our oppressors of their so-called power, and I told him no. He injected himself with serums and became a monster, destroying our lab and killing multiple scientists and government officials that day. I knew I had to take all the serums there at that very moment. Hide them along with all of our research as well. Since then, I've been running and hiding from him for years, just trying to protect the family."

He says to him. "What was his name, grandpa?"

Bernard looks at Jalen and says. "Zion Pierce is his name. Jalen, there is another thing I need to tell you. Before you were a year old. You had a terrible case of asthma. You literally had symptoms showing all day long on most days, and I gave you the serum to help give you a normal life until a day like this came."

Jalen stands up and walks around the room in shock and says. "Wait, slow down, grandpa, so you're telling me I'm like him somehow."

Bernard says to Jalen. "Jalen, listen, the serum I gave you improved everything in your body. Starting with your brain function to the immune system and your athletic abilities."

He looks at him and says. "Are there any powers that I could have that we don't know about? Okay, so all these years, I thought the way I see the basketball court was normal, and it turns out it's basically not."

He asks Jalen. "How do you normally see the court when you're playing?"

"It's kind of weird talking about it but I sometimes see angles like the whole court is one geometrical equation or something," he says to his grandpa.

Bernard says to Jalen. "Kid, I want you to think about it for a second that serum has been why you haven't got the flu or any infections in the past. I know I shouldn't have kept this from you. I'm sorry."

He then asks him a question out of curiosity. "Grandpa, it's okay, but who else knows about me having the serum in my system and your old lab partner Zion."

Bernard says to him. "You are actually the only person that knows the government covered up the whole Zion situation. I've been hiding from them because they want the serums and my research to create an army of super-soldiers to win wars that we are honestly outgunned. No one else in the family knows about this stuff."

He stands there in shock about everything and says. "It's crazy to think that I thought you were just some old nerd of a grandpa. It turns out you were this big secret scientist working on a world-breaking discovery that was weaponized, and it went left. This serum can also be used to cure sick people if you isolate the certain proteins that a person's body may need to prevent the diseases or infections."

Bernard laughs at what he says to him and then says. "Yeah, it's crazy because that's what we originally wanted to do with them. These were years ahead of any modern-day medicine. These so-called serums could have healed infected blood cells and turned somebody's body back to normal health. The government said no because they wanted to use it in the Persian Gulf War. That we had just entered at the time when we had just finished making the serums; these serums could turn soldiers with perfect health into straight living weapons."

Jalen sits back down in the chair and says to his Grandfather. "Well, what's the plan now that we know that Zion is here in Georgia."

Bernard deeply exhales and says. "I need you to fight and stop him."

He sits back in his chair and makes a face, confused with what Bernard says, and replies to him. "Grandpa, slow down real quick; what do you mean to fight and stop him."

"Like I just said, I need you to fight him and stop him from whatever he's planning," he says to Jalen.

"Hold on listening, grandpa, I can't go out there fighting crime like I'm damn batman now. I literally have no training," he says to Bernard.

He responds to Jalen by saying. "Jalen, you're the only person that can stop Zion from causing a calamity. I need you, kid; this much bigger than both you and me. If he gets his hand on the serum, there's no telling of what could happen."

"What do you need me to do, grandpa? When do we start," he asks grandpa as he makes up his mind to help?

Bernard smiles at him and says to him. "That's the thing we started when you put on that suit, actually. First, we need to find that the tracker in the suit deactivates the homing beacon. Hold on, I have to get something real quick."

Bernard walks into the supplies room and pulls out a metal detector to locate the tracker inside the suit. They spend a couple minutes trying to find it and end up finding it in the threading of the sleeve. Bernard begins to cut it open carefully, removes the tracker, throws it down, and steps on it, crushing it. The tracker is no longer active.

Jalen says to Bernard. "Aye, Grandpa, how do you expect me to go up against him with no equipment."

He smiles at him, walks over to his desk, and presses a button. The walls flip and open, revealing many weapons and gadgets and monitors.

Jalen's jaw immediately drops when he sees everything and says."Holy Shit, this is crazy right now. My nasty grandpa, I didn't mean to curse like that."

Bernard walks over to Jalen and puts his arm around him, and he begins to start showing Jae around, telling him about each piece of equipment."I told you I've been prepping for this day ever since I gave you that serum because I knew it would come to this one day, and it's okay. This is your destiny, Jae."

"Not everything on these walls has been completely updated; some of this stuff is a couple of years old with old wiring," he then mentions to Jaleen.

Jae then asks his Grandfather."Okay, how old is a couple of years to you? Because you know y'all old folk say a couple of years but end up being 10 to 12 years, but it doesn't matter. I'm gonna take a look at some of the stuff that I could use."

Bernard laughs at him and says to him. "No, it really hasn't been that long. It's only probably been like 2 to 5 years for certain things. It was really because I kept starting a new project while being in the middle of another one."

Jalen says to him."That's probably where I get that from not ultimately finishing one project entirely." Jalen then starts laughing at his own joke to Bernard.

Jalen looks around at the whole room and then says. "Grandpa, I need a suit that withstands just about anything if I go out there fighting Zion."

Bernard picks up the suit he initially took from the lab and replies to Jae, saying. "This is your suit right here. We can make a couple of essential modern modifications to give you a more modern look. I know the material is a little old, so we could switch it up, and if you want, we could upgrade it more later."

Jae looks at Bernard, shrugs his shoulders, smiles, and asks. "Okay, so where am I even going to train at Grandpa?"

Bernard looks at the wall and presses a button, and a small stairway opens up. Bernard signals Jae to come and walk with him, and they walk down the stairs to a room equivalent to the size of half of a football field.

This empty floor has nothing on it but just light on the ceilings. Bernard says to Jae. "This is where you will train yourself and work on new gear. How do you feel about that kid?"

Jalen looks amazed at everything he's seen in the last couple of minutes and then says. "Honestly, grandpa, I think we can stop him."

Shaw and his men finally show back up at the hideout. The anonymous man stands in the lair, waiting for them with his hands behind his back, glaring at them with disappointment.

Shaw looks and says. "Zion, there was a problem with the person that had the suit on; he was a kid that moved faster than me; it was almost like he was-"

Zion looks at Shaw and says. "t was almost like he was abnormal, right?"

Shaw replies back to Zion. "Yeah, how'd you know, sir."

Zion grabs Shaw and picks him up off the ground and says. "Did you get any information on him?"

Shaw looks at Zion and answers him, saying. "We didn't get anything; he was just running from us; we would capture him with the tranquilizer guns."

Zion throws Shaw down and yells at him, saying. "Wait, you shot at him in public; what is wrong with you?"

Shaw then says to him. "Pierce, I know, but he was actually the one to make a scene first, throwing hot chocolate on us and hitting us with food trays and everything."

Zion points at one of the henchmen in the hideout and tells him. "I want you to get on the computer right now. Hack into the mall Security feed and see if we can identify this kid. I need to know who he is now."

Shaw says to Zion. "Zion, if you don't mind me asking, why are you so interested in this kid?"

Zion turns around and looks at Shaw and says. "He and have the same thing running through our veins, the serums I've been looking for. He's the key to finding it, actually."

Shaw looks at Zion in shock at what he just said to him.

Zion then begins to walk over to Shaw and says to him. "Oh yeah, another, don't question me ever again. I'm your boss, and you're my flunky." Zion punches him and then grabs Tyler Shaw and throws him into a wall as a punishment.

Everyone in the hideout looks at them in fear of what just happened. Zion then says. "Anybody else got something to say? Go ahead and speak up if you want what he's having."

One of the henchmen hacking the mall security feed decided to raise his hand.

He then tells Zion, hesitantly stumbling over his words. "I hacked into their feed, and I found the footage of the altercation from earlier, sir. Dr. Pierce, I identified him as well. His name is JalenCollins; he's a junior at Northview high school with a 3.8 GPA."

Zion looks at the picture of Jalen and says. "Look up, relatives. I want you to go a little deeper on this kid."

The henchman starts looking into Jalen's family. He finds a picture of Bernard revealing that to be Jalen's Grandfather. He then pulls up his family tree of relatives related to his grandparents to great-grandparents.

Zion sees the picture of Bernard and says to the henchmen as he's scrolling through. "Wait, stop right there, Bernard, I have finally found you after all this time, and you gave your grandson the serums you stole from me. I hope he knows I'm coming for him and his grandson." Zion then walks away, laughing at what he just found out.

Later that night, Jalen gets up and goes over to Maya's house before it's too late. He gets to her house, and she opens the door and hugs him.

She immediately asks him, "Jae, are you okay? I've been worried because you weren't answering the phone, and you told me not to go to the police and report it."

Maya begins to hyperventilate because she is scared of everything that has happened before.

He grabs her hands and says. "I'm okay; there's no need to worry, okay."

She then grabs his hand, and they go and sit in her room and talk about earlier. Maya's mom walks into her room and says, "Hey Jae, how are you?"

He simply replies back to her, saying. "I'm okay, Mrs. Wilson; what about yourself?"

Mrs.Wilson looks at him and smiles, and says. "I'm doing good, sweetie."

She then points at Maya and says. "This one right here has literally been talking about you all weekend long since Friday."

He laughs and looks over at Maya and says. "Dang, was she really talking about me that much, Mrs.Wilson?"

She laughs at him and says, "Yeah, she was like me, and Jalen are going out on a little date this weekend."

Maya laughs at the both of them messing with her and then says to her mom. "Mom, can you please stop; you are legit embarrassing me right now."

Mrs.Wilson laughs at her and walks out of the room. He laughs and starts to lay on the floor.

Maya looks at him on the floor and asks him. "Jae, what really happened after you dropped me off?"

He looks at her and smiles and says. "Maya, I just need you to trust me; everything is okay."

She looks at him very curiously, and she asks him. "What did your grandfather say about everything?"

He smiles at her and says. "We went to file a police report about the whole situation, so there's really nothing for us to stress over. It's in the police hands now."

She says to Jalen. "I guess that kind of puts my mind at ease."

He then asks Maya. "What are your plans for the night?"

Maya replies to Jalen, saying. "Whatever you want to do, honestly."

He stands up and says to her. "I really wanted to just hang out with you."

Maya says to him. "Really, okay, how about we do some gingerbread houses and watch Christmas movies because it's only 7 o'clock?"

Jalen looks at her and says. "you already know I'm down for that. I low-key have been wanting to do that with you too."

The two of them get up and get ready to go to the store and buy gingerbread house kits. Then two of them come back to Maya's house. They both sit down and make gingerbread houses while watching the Christmas movie of Maya's choice, The Grinch.

Chapter 5

On December 19th, Jalen went to his grandfather's office to start training. Jalen goes inside. He sees that Bernard already has all the equipment for his training as he looks around the room, still amazed at everything he sees.

Bernard sees him walking in and asks Jalen. "What's up, Jae? I hope you're ready to start your training?"

He smiles and answers. "What's the first grandpa? Throw whatever you got at me."

Bernard looks at Jalen and says to him. "Now see, don't get ahead of yourself now; we need to start you off with the basics."

Jalen places his book bag down on Bernard's desk. Bernard opens a notebook in his hand and starts writing in it.

Jalen looks over at Bernard and notices the notebook. Jae then asks him. "Why do you have a notebook with you?"

Bernard looks up at him as he finishes writing in the notebook and says to him. "I got this to keep track of your progress as we're doing your training."

Jalen yawns and says. "Oh, okay, cool sounds good to me."

Bernard looks over and tells him. "First, you should change into your suit because that's basically your battle suit. You need to break it in and make it feel comfortable to you."

He walks over to the wall where the suit is placed, and he begins to take his clothes off to put on his suit.

He then says to his grandson. "Woah, what are you doing? I don't want to see all of that come on, man."

He laughs and says to Bernard, "My bad grandpa, I'll go over to the other room and change."

He walks into the room right over, changes into the suit, and walks back into the other room. Bernard walks over to him and grabs his wrist.

Bernard tells Jalen, "I made some modifications this morning to the suit with a new tracker that only I or you have access to. There's also a new wrist head ups display, otherwise known as your h.u.d. That will also tell you your navigation system, health, and suit damages."

He looks at him and smiles at Bernard, and says to him, "Dang, grandpa, you've been busy."

He replies to him saying. "Yeah, I guess you can say that."

He then asks Bernard. "Okay, what do you mean about the wrist hud indicating my health?"

Bernard replies to him, saying. "It will be able to tell you if you have any fractures, tears, and broken bones."He replies to him. "Okay, that's actually pretty cool, Grandpa. Okay, so you ready because I am." Jalen starts stretching with the suit on, trying to break it in.

Bernard looks over at Jalen and tells him. "We will start with combat training with the sparring dummy I made last night and finished this morning. I could only make three of them because of how little time we had."

Bernard then opens the stairwell to the training area for Jalen, and they both walk down. Bernard gets the sparring dummies down there to start combat training. He then pulls out a computer that sets up the whole training area of nanotechnology.

He afterward asks Jalen. "Are you ready to start, kid?"

He replies back to him saying. "Yeah, let's do it, Grandpa."

Bernard looks at him and says." I want to actually test your strength first and speed more than anything. I also want to check your endurance and stamina too."

Jalen exhales and asks his grandpa. "Alright, grandpa, how much do you want me to start with weight-wise; You want me to do 190, then we just keep increasing from there?"

Bernard looks at Jalen and nods his head, and says. "Yeah, that actually sounds perfect. Get the bar and go ahead, start lifting."

Bernard starts keeping track of Jae's strength as it increases to find out his limits. He lifts weights for thirty minutes and increases his strength to eight hundred pounds. He then starts bench-pressing the consequences.

He does one last set of the 800 and says to Bernard. "Yeah, that's it; that's my max right there. I can't lift anymore."

Bernard says to Jalen. "Jae, you lifted 800, so that's outstanding. So let's go ahead and test your speed now, kid. Okay, I want to see how fast you are on a 40-yard dash."

"Okay, grandpa, I'm ready whenever you are. "Jalen says to Bernard as he tries to catch his breath from lifting those weights.

Bernard then sets up the training area for Jae's speed and endurance testing with nanotech.

He then says to him. "Jae, let's get started on your speed test."

Jae nods his head and gets his feet set to run. He takes off from the start marker and runs an astonishing 2.5 on his 40-yard dash. Bernard then looks at the results from Jae's sprint and sees that he ran 50 miles per hour.

Bernard implies to him. "Jae, your speed is amazing; you ran 50 miles per hour, dude." He then high fives Jalen and smiles at him.

Jalen then gets a towel and sits down. He then relaxes and drinks some water.

Bernard looks over and says. "Jae, we're going to take a 20 minutes break, and then we could start your sparring, okay."

Jalen lays down on the floor and gives his grandpa a thumbs up, indicating that he understands him.

Bernard then activates the sparring dummies and starts having Jalen do some regular jabs at the dummies. He does that for a couple of minutes, then Bernard makes the dummies fight back to help Jalen work on defending himself, and he fights them to just practice. Jalen ends up practicing his defensive fighting for a whole 3 hours learning to become a better fighter, and focuses on dodging punches and kicks first. Afterward, he focuses on his counterattacks on an enemy. Jalen then takes a break and goes upstairs to Bernards's office and gets some water and a quick bite to eat. As he is upstairs, he stands in front of the wall with the gadgets and the wrist darts.

Bernard walks up to him and stands next to him, and says. "Yeah, I know it's a lot of stuff on this wall."

Jalen says to grandpa. "Aye, Grandpa, when will I be able to train with all of those things up there."

The next day, Bernard grabs some of the gadgets and the wrist darts, walks down to the training room, and says. "I hope you're ready to learn weapon training today, kid."

Jalen Begins to walk down, smiles at Bernard, and puts the wrist darts on.

He points the darts at the sparring dummies and says. "Okay, grandpa, now how do I even shoot them?"

Bernard says to Jalen. "Try making a complete fist and see if that signals it to discharge the darts."

Jalen then tries to do what his grandfather tells him to do. He shoots 3 darts at the sparring dummies, and as the darts begin to discharge from the wrist holder. Jalen yells with excitement, and he and Bernard look at each other and start laughing.

The two of them spend the next few days training. Jalen starts getting better with his fighting. Bernard starts increasing the difficulty of the sparring dummies to push him to get stronger and faster. Jae gets a little banged up from the dummies fighting back.

Jalen gets exhausted from training as he realizes he has bruises on his body. He then says. "Grandpa, I got to take a break; we have been going at this since 8 this morning; it's like 3 o'clock now."

Bernard shuts down the sparring drones and says. "Jae, I know I'm sorry I just want you to be ready for Zion when you meet him and have to stop him."

Jalen walks upstairs to Bernard's office. Bernard walks up the stairs, enters his office, and says. "Jae, I just want you to know you have been showing a lot of progress, and I'm so proud." He then walks over to the refrigerator and gets water.

Jalen takes a sip from his water and replies to him, saying. "Yeah, I know, Grandpa, it's just a lot. I feel like I'm in a comic book right now."

He laughs at Jalen and says. "What superhero would you compare your training to right now if you could then?"

He wipes his face with his towel and sipes his water again. He then tells his grandfather, "Honestly, grandpa, I couldn't even tell you because every story is different in its own way."

Bernard looks at him and laughs again, and says to him. "That's actually very understandable, Jae its okay."

Jalen then laughs at his grandpa and says. "Yeah, but one thing for sure is that you are most definitely Alfred."

The two of them enjoy the rest of the day by doing some light training and working on some new equipment. Jalen notices that his bruises are starting to heal, and They begin to realize that Jalen has a healing factor from reading the vitals on his suit.

The next day he comes over to the office to train. Bernard makes a couple of modifications to the suit and tests Jae's healing factor to see its limitations.

Bernard takes the suit off the wall after installing new tech to it, and he looks over at Jalen and says. "You want to take the suit out for a spin and stroll the rooftops."

He looks and smirks at him and replies. "Okay, that would be pretty cool, but how would I even get around the city from rooftop to rooftop."

He then responds to him by saying."I have 4 prototypes of grappling darts that you could use to get around. They were in development for when I first made the wrist darts."

Jalen replies to his grandfather by saying. "Okay, how many times were they tested in the field?"

Bernard looks down and says. "Well, that's the thing, Jae, we actually never got a chance to do a field test for all the equipment except for the suit. Which I forgot to mention is bulletproof? It's coated with nanotechnology that helps absorb the kinetic energy from any attacks to bounce it back at your opponents on command."

Jalen looks at Grandpa and says sarcastically. "Okay, you know what, grandpa, that actually really helps a lot. What if I fight, and none of this stuff works for me?"

Bernard says to Jalen. "Yeah, I know it doesn't really help. I'm sorry."

He says to Bernard. "Wait, Grandpa, how did you even come up with all this stuff? This is honestly crazy."

Bernard says to him. "Yeah, I know I've spent years researching and preparing for a time like this."

Bernard opens up the roof for Jalen to leave and test the equipment. Jalen then starts to get ready to stroll around the town. Jalen goes up to the roof and begins his first stroll.

Jalen then says to him. "Okay, grandpa, where should I go to give all the equipment a full field test."

Bernard tells him. "Take a full rooftop run and try out the grappling dart and remember to be careful because they're prototypes. Put this in your ear so we can communicate back and forth."

He puts the earpiece in his ear and heads up to the roof. He then starts looking around on the rooftops and figuring out where to run. He then says to Bernard. "Damn, grandpa, it's low-key cold out here; this wind is ridiculous."

Bernard laughs and says to him. "Yeah, you know I just added something for you too."

Jalen stands on the rooftop shivering and asks. "What'd you add to the suit, grandpa."

Bernard activates the heater in the suit for him to keep him warm.

Jalen then asks Bernard. "Grandpa, what did you just do because my suit is getting warmer."

Bernard chuckles and says to Jae. "Nothing, I just activated the heater in your suit; it also has a cooling feature. The suit will turn off the heater or cooling feature when your body temperature has returned to normal."

He laughs and says to him. "Grandpa, you're something else coming up with these new modifications. Okay, grandpa, I'm ready to let's do this."

Grandpa smiles, puts navigation on Jalen's wrist hud, and says, "Okay, Jae, I put the navigation up. Now go ahead and give this suit a spin."

He looks down at the wrist hud and begins to run towards the navigation and move from building to building, showing off his agility. He then tries the grappling dart, and it successfully goes through a wall but doesn't retract itself for him to go up the building. Jalen runs freely across the city's rooftops with a bright and warm smile.

He begins to hang from the building and tells his grandfather. "Yeah, grandpa, the grappling dart has to be tested again."

Jalen then climbs the rope of the grapple. He stands on the roof, looks around the city, and tells Bernard. "You have to see this view, grandpa; it's unbelievable up here, and you could see everything from here."

Bernard smiles and says to Jae over the com-link. "Well, come on, back training is done for the day."

He laughs and then says. "Okay, I'm coming back right now." Jalen then runs and front-flips off the building and lands on another building.

A couple of minutes pass by. Jalen gets back to the facility with his grandpa and starts to his gear off and put it on the wall.

"Now that your training is over for the day, what will you do for the rest of the day?" Bernard asks him as he starts gathering his stuff to leave.

He then looks at his grandfather and says. "Honestly, grandpa, it's only like 4 o'clock right now, so I might take Maya out somewhere I still haven't decided."

Bernard chuckles and replies back. "Here, take this, so if you do, take her out." He then walks over to his wallet sitting on top of his desk. Bernard reaches inside his wallet and gives Jalen a hundred dollars.

Jalen looks at the money and says. "No, I can't take that, grandpa."

Bernard smiles at him and hands him the money, and says. "No, take the money, kid; it's for you because we have been training nonstop."

Jalen takes the money and puts it in his backpack. "Are you sure, grandpa? "He then asks his grandfather.

"Yes, Jae, I want you to go out and have fun for a couple of days because we're not going to train for the next 2 days," said Bernard to Jalen.

He then asks him. "Dang, why not?"

He responds back to him, indicating. "It will be Christmas Eve and Christmas, so enjoy your next couple of days off from training. I wouldn't have you train on Christmas and eve and Christmas, kid."

Jalen laughs at Bernard and says. "Alright, grandpa, I'm going to see you later."

Bernard and Jalen dap each other up, and he walks out of the facility. Jalen then puts his stuff in his car. Jalen gets in his car and turns it on, and drives off. After driving down the road for a couple minutes and he arrives at home. Jalen then goes inside the house with his stuff and takes a nap.

He wakes up from his nap and questions himself."Damn, how long was I asleep?"

He then looks down at his phone and sees that Maya called him once and texted him twice and realizes it's now 9 o'clock, indicating he slept for a couple of hours. He then chooses to go out and do something tomorrow on Christmas Eve with Maya.

Maya then calls Jalen. He answers the phone, and he and Maya start talking.

Maya asks Jae. "What's up, Jae?"

"Nothing; what's up with you?" Jae asks Maya as he really starts to wake up.

"How was your day because I barely even spoke to you today?" Maya then asks him as she combs her hair on FaceTime with him.

"My bad, I was just busy helping my grandpa out today," he said to her.

"Yeah, I understand but come to think about it, we haven't been speaking like that the last couple of days," she says to him, and she stops combing her hair.

"Yeah, I'm sorry," he said to Maya.

"Jae, I need you to be honest with me; if you don't want to try this with me, we don't have to, and we could go back to normal and just stick to being friends," she then says to him concerned about the two of them.

He exhales and says to her. "Wait, what are you talking about because I'm lost now?"

She goes back to combing her hair and answers him. "Jalen, I now just feel like you're playing with my feelings at this point."

He looks into the phone at Maya and says to her, giving her a sign of reassurance. "Look, Maya, I'm sorry I've just been busy with my grandpa the last couple of days. I should've told you I was going to be busy. Can I please make it up to you tomorrow?"

Maya looks down at the phone and asks." Okay, but what are we going to do then?"

He laughs and smiles at her and asks Maya. "What about ice skating because I know that you've always wanted to do it?"

Maya continues to comb her hair and smiles and asks. "Really, what time do you want to go?"

"How about I come to pick you up at six o'clock? We could go get something to eat, and then we could go ice skating," he then asks her how she feels about the plans for tomorrow.

Maya smiled into the phone and said. "Yeah, I like that, and don't be late this time either."

Jalen smiles and laughs with Maya on the phone. The two of them spend the next couple of hours talking and fall asleep on the phone.

Jalen wakes up in the morning, and Maya tells him when she wakes up. "Jae, I will call you later, okay, and let you know I'm getting ready."

He replies to her. "Okay, Maya, I will let you know when I'm on the way."

A couple of hours go by, and Jalen starts getting ready to head out with Maya. He pulls out his phone as he gets ready to leave his house.

Jae calls Maya on the phone and says. "I'm about to leave and be on the way."

She smiles into the phone and says. "Okay, I'm almost ready; just let me know when you get here."

Jalen hangs up the phone, walks downstairs, and grabs his keys   off of the kitchen counter. He walks out the front door, gets in his vehicle, and lets it warm up first. He then backs out of the driveway and goes to the store to pick up some roses for Maya. Jalen picks up the roses, self-checkout, and pays for the roses there. He then gets in his car and heads over to Maya's house to pick her up.

When he arrived at her house, he texted her saying. "Hey, I'm outside. I just got here."

She then replies to him, saying. "Okay, I'll be down; just come to the door in a second."

He turns his car off, gets out with the roses in his hand, and heads towards Maya's front door. He then gets to the door and puts the roses behind his back to hide them from her. When he reaches his arm out to knock on the door, Maya opens the door. The two look at each other and smile immediately. Jalen gazes at her and says. "Damn, you look perfect right now."

Maya smiles and says. "You don't look bad yourself."

He takes the roses from his back, gives them to Maya, and says. "These are for you, Maya."

Maya smiles and smells the roses and says to Jalen. "Wow, Jalen, these are really nice; thank you."

"No problem, I was just like, why not because this our first real date," he said to her as they stood speaking in front of the door.

She then kisses him on the cheek and says. "Hold on real quick. I'm going to put this inside."

Jalen smiles at her and nods his head. She walks into the house and puts the flowers down on a table. She then comes back outside, and as she closes the front door, she asks him. "Hey, you are ready to go?"

He then responds to her question by saying. "Yeah, let's get going, honestly."

The two of them walk to the car, and he opens Maya's door for her to get in the vehicle. Jalen turns the car on, and they leave Maya's house. After driving on the road for 20 minutes, they arrive at an Italian restaurant and get something to eat before ice skating. The two of them sit down at the restaurant and talk.

He sits across from Maya browsing the menu and asks her. "What are you thinking about getting because mostly everything looks and sounds good on here?"

"I don't know because the shrimp and scallop fettuccine Alfredo sounds real good," Maya says to him. They both continue to browse over the menu.

The Waiter comes out with 2 baskets of bread, one with rolls and one with breadsticks.

Jae grabs and puts 2 rolls on his plate, and Maya puts 3 breadsticks on her plate. Jalen eats his roll and looks at the menu and says." I'm probably going to get the spinach and chicken tortellini pasta."

Maya says to him. "I think I know what I want now, too; I'm leaning towards the shrimp and scallop fettuccine Alfredo with some spinach added in."

Jalen laughs, and Maya asks him, "Wait, what is tortellini Jae?"

He smiles and says to her. "They're like ravioli noodles but not; it's hard to explain, but I'll let you try them when they come out."

She smiles at Jalen and says to him. "Okay, but don't think you'll get some of my food just because you shared yours."

"Damn, it's like that, wow," he asks her as he starts laughing at her.

"Mhm yeah, it's like that," she replies to him as they're both laughing.

Jalen waves down the Waiter so they can order their food. The Waiter walks over and asks them, "Hey, are you guys ready to order now?"

Maya looks up at the Waiter and says. "Yeah, we are all ready, sir."

The Waiter then takes out his notepad to write down Jalen and Maya's order and asks them, "Okay, what could I get you for, guys?"

Maya looks down at the menu and says. "Okay, I think going to get the shrimp and scallop fettuccine."

The Waiter begins writing on the notepad and says, "Okay, that is really good here."

Maya says to the Waiter, "Okay, good because it sounded real and looks good."

The Waiter then asks Jalen. "Okay, what can I get for you, sir?"

Maya asks The Waiter. "Wait can I get some spinach added to the pasta, please?"

The Waiter starts writing down what Maya asks and says. "Yeah, I can definitely add that in for you."

"Okay, cool," said Maya to the Waiter as he added something to her order.

The Waiter asks Jalen. "Now, what can I get you, sir?"

Jalen looks down at the menu and says to him. "I'm going to get the spinach and chicken tortellini pasta."

The Waiter writes down Jae's order and says to him."Okay, I got you. I'm going to put this in now."

The Waiter walks away to put the orders in for Maya and Jalen.

20 minutes go by, and their food comes out, and two of them start eating their food.

Maya then asks Jalen. "Wait, Jae, remember you said I can try some?"

He chuckles and says to her. "Yeah, I remember to go ahead and try some. I think you're going to like it."

Maya then takes her fork out, puts a little bit of Jalen's pasta on her plate, tries it, and says. "Damn, I should have gotten this because this is really good."

He begins to tell her after seeing her reaction to trying his food. "See, I told you it would be good, but you didn't believe me."

They smile at each other and continue to eat their food. Time passes, and the two finish their food at the restaurant and leave. They then head over to the ice skating rink.

When they get there, he says to Maya. "I've never ice skated before, so don't laugh at me if I fall."

Maya then starts laughing at him and asks. "You know this will be my first time on the ice, right?"

"Yeah, I know, but you're super confident like you're a pro at this," he said to her as they began to get out of the car.

The two walk into Icicle, the ice skating rink, and rent the skates to skate. They both put on their skates, head onto the ice, and fall immediately. They both start laughing at each other and get right back up and fall again. After that, they then decide to skate by holding onto the wall to prevent them from falling.

As the two of them skate on the ice while holding the wall. Maya asks Jalen. "Can I ask you a question real quick?"

"Yeah, I just got to make sure I don't fall though," Jalen says to her as he looks at her and holds onto the wall.

"Jae, so what really made you want to go ice skating and actually, you know, take me out on a date," she asks Jalen as the two of them continue to skate.

"Well, I owe you an apology for how I have been acting this week with barely talking to you," he says to her as he moves staggering across the ice.

Maya looks over at Jalen and says how she feels. "If that's the case, I accept your apology, but you can just speak to me next time. We have been friends since elementary school."

They both stop skating, and he looks at her and says. "I know I should have said something, but now I know I can from now on."

Maya reaches in to hug Jalen, and he starts losing his balance. He tries to regain his balance and falls down while holding Maya's hand. The both of them fall down on the ice and start laughing.

About an hour and a half pass by, and they get ready to leave the ice skating rink. The two go to put the skates back, and they get stuck under a mistletoe. The lady at the skate rental counter tells them. "Just kiss already; it's mistletoe."

They both smile, and they both lean in for a kiss. Maya's phone rings, and it's her mom calling her.

Maya then answered the phone and said to her mom on the phone. "Hey, mom, we're actually getting ready to leave the ice skating place, so I should be home in a little while."

Maya's mom then says, "Okay, please be careful on the way back."

Jae and Maya then get in the car and head back to Maya's house to drop her off. He arrives at her house, walks her to the door, and says. "You know Maya, I had a perfect time with you tonight, and I hope we can keep doing this."

She smiles and asks him. "Keep doing what exactly?"

Jalen laughs and says to her. "Like keep going on dates with you."

She replies to him with. "Oh, I would like that because I enjoy spending time with you."

Jalen leans into Maya to go for the kiss, and her mom comes and opens the door. Maya's mom says to her. "Maya, when you come in, make sure you lock up completely, and Jalen, please let Maya know you made it back home because it is late out here."

Jalen smiles and says to her. "Yes, ma'am, I surely will."

Maya nods her head at her mom, letting her know she understands. She tells Jalen, "I gotta go, so give me a hug real quick."

Jalen reaches in for a hug, and the two lock eyes once more and finally kiss. After the kiss, Maya walks into the house smiling, locks the door, and goes to her room. Jalen walks to his car, smiles, gets in, and heads home.

Fifteen minutes later, he gets to his house, goes to his room, and sets his keys and phone down on his nightstand. Jalen sits down on his bed, unties his shoes, and takes his clothes off. He then grabs his phone on his nightstand and says to himself. "Let me go ahead and text Maya and let her know I made it home." He begins to text Maya that he made it home, turns on the tv, and lays down to sleep.

The next day Jalen wakes up, and it's Christmas. Jalen checks his phone when he wakes up, and there are a couple of messages from people saying Merry Christmas to him. Jalen texts his brother, grandfather, Justin, and Maya and says Merry Christmas to them all. Jalen gets out of bed, uses the bathroom, and brushes his teeth. Jalen goes back into his room, grabs his phone, and walks downstairs. As soon as he gets down the steps, he smells food and sniffs the air. He walks into the kitchen and sees that his parents cooked a massive breakfast for Christmas. He goes and gets a plate out of the cabinet and starts making himself a plate. Jalen's brother Robert and his family come over. Jalen's grandma soon arrives shortly after Robert. Bernard comes over as well, and they all start sitting in the house, opening presents and eating breakfast as a family. The guys sit in the living room and watch the Christmas NBA games and talk.

A couple of hours pass by, and the doorbell rings; Lisa opens the door, and its Maya at the door.

"Hey everybody, Merry Christmas," Maya says to everyone as she walks through the door at Jalen's house.

Jalen then comes downstairs, walks over to Maya, and hugs her.

Jalen's grandma smiles at them and says. "It's about time y'all two are dating. I've been waiting to see y'all two together for the last four years."

Jalen laughs nervously and asks. "Wait, grandma, what are you talking about?"

Maya says to Jae's grandma, "Yeah, grandma, nothing is going on here; we're just friends."

Lisa Collins looks at them both and says, "Mhm, we all know y'all are into each other it's okay."

Maya and Jalen look at each other and smile. Jalen then asks her." Are you hungry because my parents made a whole bunch of food?"

Maya nods her head and says to him. "Yeah, I'm actually starving. I haven't since we went to dinner last night."

He shakes his head in disbelief and says to her. "Yo, you are crazy as hell. I couldn't dare do that, twelve hours with no food." The two walk into the kitchen so she can make a plate for hers.

She laughs and says to him. "Leave me alone; I just have a slow metabolism."

Jalen laughs at her and says. "Well, we have a lot of everything; we got bacon, sausage, eggs, French toast, and pancakes."

Maya peaks out of the kitchen into the living room and says to Jalen's parents. "Okay, Mr. and Mrs. Collins, you all threw down in the kitchen today."

Lisa laughed and said to her. "Yeah, you better dig in while you still can."

Maya smiles at her and laughs, and says. "Oh yeah, I'm making a full plate with everything."

Jalen laughs and starts making another plate with sausage, pancakes, and French toast. Maya and Jalen both warm their food and sit down and eat their food together at the table. Some time goes by, and the two of them finish their food. He gets up and throws both of their plates away. When Jalen goes to the kitchen, his grandfather is in there.

Bernard tells Jalen quietly in the kitchen. "They're a break in being reported at one of the tech facilities in the city we need to go. I just got the alarm on my phone from a police report."

He looks at his grandfather, perplexed, and asks him. "Why, what does that have to do with me actually?"

He steps closer to Jae and says."Jalen thinks, this probably Zion trying to make his move for whatever he needs for his plans."

He nods his head and asks him." Okay, so what are we going to tell everybody because we need an excuse for why we are leaving?"

"Shit, I didn't even think about that at all, but I come with something on the fly, so don't worry about it," he then replies to him about the plan.

Jalen says to Bernard's they agree on the plan." Okay, let me go talk to Maya and let her know I have to run out with you."

He then walks to Maya and says. "Please don't get mad."

Maya asks Jalen as she starts to get anxious. "What are you talking about? What happened?"

Jalen takes a deep breath and says to Maya." I have to run to the office real quick with grandpa; he's getting some alarms, some we have to check the system and everything."

She looks at him and simply says to him calmly. "Jae, it's okay. I understand; thank you for letting me know; I'll just sit here with the rest of your family and have fun."

She then pulls Jalen closer to her, smiles at his face, and kisses him.

Jalen smiles and walks and says. "I will be back in like three hours tops; it's 530 now. I should be back no later than 9, okay." Maya nods her head at him. Bernard tells the family as everybody sits there in the living room." Jae and I have to run to the office and check the alarms because they're going off, and everything will be over there for a couple of hours."

Lisa Collins says to her dad as he breaks the news to everyone quickly. "Okay, y'all be careful out there because you know people have been drinking and partying; it is the holidays."

Jalen looks at his mom and says. "Okay, we will later, you guys; we will be back soon." Bernard and Jalen open the door, walk out of the house, get in Jalen's car, and drive to Bernard's office.

Chapter 6

The two of them arrive at Bernard's office, hop out of the car, and run into the office. The two of them sit down to access the computers to locate the break-in.

Bernard looks at the computer and says."Jae, go ahead and suit up."

Jalen walks to the wall where his suit is and grabs it off the wall. Jae then puts it on along with his gear. He looks at Bernard and nods his head at him.

Bernard looks up at him and says."Before I forget, I made this mask for you as well; it's connected to the hud on your wrist."

Bernard grabs the mask off his workstation and hands it to Jalen.

He then grabs the mask from his grandfather and just looks at it.

Bernard looks at him and says. "The lens in your mask will show your navigation and heat signatures, and I also synced your phone with it."

Jalen then puts on the mask and says back to him." Wait, grandpa, I can't see anything at all."

Bernard looks at him and says." Wait, hold on, let me sync everything together."

"Okay, grandpa," he says as he waits for him.

He says to him as he finally sends the signal for the mask to work. "Okay, look, the mask should be coming online right now."

The lens in the mask then opens up, and Jalen can see through the lens and says. "Oh yeah, grandpa, I could see everything now."

Bernard smiles at Jalen and says to him. "Perfect, that's what I want to hear."

He starts walking up the stairs to the roof.

Right before he goes on to the roof, Bernard says to him. "Jae listens to me; this could be our only chance at stopping Zion; I need you to please be careful."

He looks at him and says."I'm going to try my best, grandpa; I know this will be crazy."

He then tells him. "Now get going, Jae, and end whatever plan he has."

Jae heads to the rooftop, and Bernard puts the navigation on to the HUD for him. Jalen then begins to travel to the facility's location that Zion broke into.

Jalen spends a couple of minutes going from rooftop to rooftop. He then gets to the location of the robbery. He looks from the rooftop as he sees Zion's men loading up two equipment trucks.

He then says to his grandpa. "Grandpa, I'm here, but I think I'm too late."

Bernard sits at his chair, watching everything that Jalen can see through his lenses and says. "Jae, I need you to get a little closer so I can see what they have."

Jalen continues to look on the roof and says to Bernard. "Okay, I'm going to try my best, grandpa."

"Go ahead and look for a ventilation system on the roof," Bernard says to him as he sits at his computer, guiding Jalen.

He searches around the roof for a vent to enter the building, and he then finds a skylight window and says."Grandpa, I don't see a vent on the roof, but I know a skylight window."

"Damn, since you don't see a vent go inside through there," said Bernard to Jalen as he tried to navigate him.

Jalen walks up to the roof entrance and opens it to access the building. When he gets inside the building, he sees Zion's militia walking around the premises stealing ridiculous amounts of equipment. Jalen then tries to sneak down to the ground level to see what they take from the facility.

Bernard looks through Jalen's lenses, sees them loading up machine parts, and asks himself, "What is the planning?"

Jalen sees them closing the truck's doors and getting in, beginning to leave.

He then implies to Bernard."Grandpa, they're about to leave."

Bernard then says to him."Jalen, go after them now. I need you to follow them."

The truck's engines turn on, and they start to leave the building. Then Jalen chases after the car, and he jumps onto the top of a truck. Jalen stays on the truck, and they drive back to their hideout.

After being on the truck for minutes and finally arriving in Zion's hideout, Jalen sneaks around the facility to see if he can find out about his plans.

Bernard says to him."Jae, I need you to be very careful because Zion is a volatile person."

Jalen looks around, taking cover and hiding so he won't be spotted. He whispers to Bernard. "Yeah, I know Grandpa; this place is crawling with his people."

Jalen starts to move around, sneak behind things, and try to locate a computer to find his plans. Jalen stumbles into a server room, where he finds out that there's a computer deep in the back of the server room.

He then tells Bernard. "Grandpa, I'm here in front of this huge computer."

Bernard looks at Jalen's lenses and says. "Okay, I need you to look through the system and look for any schematics."

Jalen starts typing and whispers to Bernard."Okay, I'm on it right now."

Jae searches through the computer; starts opening each file to see what he can find. Jalen spends minutes searching and stumbles upon a file called "Cloudburst." Jalen goes through the file and sees a machine initially designed to distribute antigens and cures on a mass scale, intending to cure diseases across a wide area, even entire cities. Zion plans to use it to disperse the serum over the city to evolve mankind.

Jalen looks at the computer monitor and asks."Are you seeing this?"

Bernard gasped and said to him."Jae, you need to get out of there right now."

Jalen tries to copy the files, and then he hears static in his earpiece and questions himself."What is going on right now?"

Bernard stands up out of his seat, yells, and asks him."Jae, can you hear me?"

Bernard then loses complete connection to Jalen.

Jalen starts touching his earpiece and asks him. "Grandpa, can you hear me hello?"

One of Zion's henchmen walks to Zion and tells him." Sir, there's a disturbance in the server room."

Zion gets up from his chair and says."Shaw, get a couple of your men and meet me in the server room."

Zion starts making his way to the server room, walking through the hallways of the hideout. Jalen keeps going through files on the computer until he hears footsteps approaching the room. He then finds a place to hide in the server room. Zion and his henchmen all enter the server room and search around for any intruders.

Bernard then says to Jalen. "Jae, you need to get out of there. I think he knows you're there."

Jalen, barely being able to hear Bernard and responds back to him by asking. "Wait, who are you talking about?"

Bernard says back to Jalen. "I'm talking about Zion."

Jalen then starts to panic a little bit and whispers into the com-link."Okay, I just have to figure out a way to get out of here without being detected.

Jalen starts sneaking around the server room to leave out of there. Zion continues to search the server room when he hears Jalen whispering to Bernard into the com-link. Zion looks and listens closely to the whispers and finds Jalen. He immediately grabs him and picks him up by his neck. Zion throws him across the server room. Jalen gets up, coughing.

Shaw and his men finally walk into the server room and tell Zion."I can take care of him, sir."

Zion looks at Shaw and walks toward Jalen slowly. He then cracks his knuckles and says to Shaw."No, I can use the workouts, so stay out of my way."

Jalen stands up, gets ready to fight Zion, and says to Bernard. "Hey, G, he's here, and he looks really pissed."

"Jalen gets out of there right now; you can't beat him one on one," Bernard said as he looked through his lens.

Zion starts to run full speed at Jalen and tackles him into a wall. Jalen's back crashes into a cement wall. Zion puts his forearm into his throat and smiles diabolically in his face.

Zion then says to him."So I finally get to meet you, huh, Jalen, grandson of Bernard."

Jalen groans in pain and says to him as he struggles to speak."I guess so."

Zion rips Jalen's mask off and says to him. "Bernard, you send a kid to stop me because you're not man enough to do it yourself."

Zion puts more pressure on Jalen's throat, and Jalen screams in agony. Bernard listens to Jalen screaming in pain and starts tearing up because he can't do anything.

Jalen tries to kick Zion in the chest and says."Get off of me."

Zion then throws Jalen into a computer server. Jalen gets up and shoots his wrist, and darts at Zion. Zion dodges them, runs to him, and punches him. He then coughs up blood, drops to his knees, and holds his stomach.

He walks around Jalen and looks down at him, and says."You know it's crazy that you and I are alike."

He chuckles and asks him."How is that so?"

Zion picks him up by his throat and says."That serum you have running through your bones and blood is very similar to the one that runs through mine."

He looks at him in his eyes and says. "We are not the same; my grandfather told me how you trying to sell the serum to the black market to create super soldiers."

Zion punches Jae in his ribs, throws him into a wall, and says. "Although that is true, I was also going to sell it to communities and help create the power they need to fight back against their corrupt oppressors. I want to help mankind evolve; that is my mission now."

A part of the wall falls down onto Jalen, and he struggles to get up from the rubble.

Jalen coughs from all the pain he's been feeling in his back and ribs and questions Zion."So, you were trying to start a civil war?"

Zion smiles and starts to walk toward him and says. "Precisely, I wanted to make things equal for everyone in a way."

He gets up from underneath the rubble and says to him. "Now, how would a group of super-soldiers create a change? You could be giving a criminal with bad intentions a serum."

He then smirks and looks at Jae, and says. "This country is so divided; someone your age will never understand that."

Jae coughs and just stands there looking at him.

He laughs and says."That was my plan, but due to time, things have changed, and I have even changed as well."

Jalen just stands there and stares at Zion and asks him."Well, what does that mean?"

Zion chuckles and walks near him and says."I'm going to tell you my plan because you're not going to stop me. You're a kid, and if you were to get in my way again, I would kill without even hesitating."

He looks up at him and starts coughing, trying to ignore the pain in his ribs and back.

Zion looks at him and says. "So I've built a machine originally designed to distribute antigens and cures on a mass scale. Intending to cure diseases across a wide area, even entire cities, by dispersing it into the air and eliminating the viruses in minutes."

Jalen laughs and asks him. "You're referring to the cloudburst?"

He looks shocked as he says."Exactly it seems you snooped through our computer system."

He then punches Jae in his face for snooping through their system, and he goes flying like 10 feet back.

Jalen then spits out blood. Zion walks over to Jae, picks him up, leans him on the wall, and starts an attack with punches to his midsection. Zion picks him up and throws him into the doors of the server room. Jalen then crawls down the hallway with blood leaking from his mouth. Jae has a bruise on his left cheek and a cut on the right side of his forehead. Zion then walks down the hallway, slowly following after Jalen.

Zion cracks his knuckles, walks up to him, grabs him, picks him up, and asks him."Where did you think you were going?"

He then throws him into a stack of wooden pallets at the end of the hallway.

He then crawls out of the stack of pallets and coughs up more blood, and can barely lift his arm.

He then whispers into his com-link and says. "Grandpa, can you hear me?"

Bernard sits up in his chair and says. "Yeah, I can hear you."

"I need to get out of here, gramps," he said to grandfather as he stood there in pain.

Bernard then says to him. "Tap the wrist gauntlets together; it will create a smoke cloud; use that to get out of there and come back here."

Jae stands up and looks Zion in his eyes from down the hall. He then taps his gauntlets together, and a smoke cloud appears, and he escapes Zion's hideout. Zion then runs into the shadow of smoke, and Jalen is wholly gone.

Jalen runs outside, and he grapples to the roof of a building across the street and then travels from rooftop to rooftop to get back across town to his grandfather's office.

After traveling across the city with multiple injuries, he tries to jump from another building to another one. He doesn't make it across and falls down onto the fire escape and grabs onto the rail with one arm because his other shoulder is dislocated. He then has to climb up the fire escape with his one arm and continues to run across the city trying to make it back and eventually does. He gets to the roof of the office building and walks down the stairs to get inside, and immediately falls down onto the floor.

Bernard walks into the room and says. "Jae, I'm right here."

Jae starts to take the suit off and just lays there bleeding and bruised up. Bernard picks him up and gets him into a chair, and tries to clean his wounds.

Bernard goes and gets some ice and says. "Computer, can you give me a reading on his vitals."

An image of Jalen's bone structure pops up on the computer screen. The photos show a dislocated shoulder and four broken ribs, and minor bruises on his face.

He groans in pain, thinking about all of his injuries and breaking down even though his body is slowly regenerating to 100 percent.

Bernard looks over at him and says."Jae, what's wrong? What happened?"

He stands up and says to him. "Grandpa, all of this is wrong. I don't think I could do this."

He looks confused at what he says and questions him. "What do you mean Jae?"

He looks down and shakes his head, and says."I'm in pain, grandpa, and I can't beat that man."

He then says to him."We know his plan, and now we see why he's here so we can come up with a plan to stop it; we know about the cloudburst; we have the advantage."

Jalen gets upset and says. "You're really not understanding what I'm saying."

He looks at him and indicates that he doesn't. "I guess I'm not, so break it down."

He chuckles and looks at him and says. "I don't give a damn about that cloudburst. I just got my ass kicked, and I have broken bones."

He looks at him and asks."So what are you saying?"

Jalen smirks and says." What are you not getting, old man? I could have possibly died tonight?"

Bernard looks at him and says."You weren't because I wasn't going to let that happen, and Jae, you have a healing factor. Your body is still healing your injuries now; there's no telling of how your healing factor works."

Jalen chuckles and says." Grandpa, listen to yourself; I was coughing up blood; he could have killed me, and you wouldn't have been able to do anything. You were on the whole other side of the city."

Bernard exhales and says. "Jae, he wasn't going to kill you. That wasn't his intention; they were to use you to get to me."

Jalen laughs and says to him. "Oh, now is that supposed to make me feel better."

Bernard looks and replies to him. "That's not what I meant; okay, I was just saying like everything is okay now."

Jalen smirks and says. "I'm not trying to be bait between the two of you. I'm done this, man."

Bernard says to him. "Jae, come on, please don't give up on this. "

He exhales and tells his grandfather. "Dude, this winter break was supposed to be super simple. I was supposed to just hang out with Maya and see where things go."

Bernard chuckles and says."Jalen, the girl loves you, and everyone knows that it. This thing with Zion is so much bigger than you, me, and Maya. I need you, Jae; please don't give up on this."

He looks at Bernard, walks up to him, and firmly tells him. "I quit, old man. I'm not meant to do this hero thing so let me just be a kid."

Bernard looks at him and says. "We need to stop, Zion. I need your help for real."

Jalen starts changing his clothes and throws his combat suit onto the other side of the room. Jalen turns around, grabs his car keys off the desk, and completely walks out of the office building. He walks to his car, limping while holding his ribs and groaning in pain. Jalen gets in his car, turns it on, sits there, and starts crying from the pain Zion has caused him. He then wipes his tears away.

He then calls Maya and asks her."Hey, Maya, are you still over at my house."

She then replies back to him saying." No, my mom needed me to come back to help her with something."

He says to her." Damn, I'm sorry if I took too long with grandfather."

Maya then says to him. "Jae, it's okay. I'm not upset because I got to sit there with your family and enjoy myself."

He begins to exhale and says. " Maya, look, I told my grandpa no more work for the rest of winter break because I want to make time for Maya and me."

She then looks at him through the phone and says."Dang Jae, what made you say that to him."

He looks down at his arm braced on his rib cage and replies. "I just feel like I'm slowly messing things up with you and trying to help my grandpa. The thing is, I decided to choose what's more important to me at the moment."

She smiles into the phone and says to Jalen. "Wow, Jae, I'm really shocked you said that to him."

He laughs and says back to her. "Yeah, I know, and now that I know there are no more distractions, we could finally enjoy our winter break together."

She laughs at him and says."Okay, I'm going to hold you to that."

Jalen laughs and says to her."Okay, I got you."

Maya replies back to him and says."Well, goodnight Jae. I'm about to go to sleep. I'm exhausted from today, and tell your parents to thank you for having me, and the food was great."

He then says to her. "I feel you. I'm tired, too, and I will definitely tell them you said that."

Jalen finally drives away, leaving his grandfather's office and going home. After minutes of driving down the road with no music in the car, he arrives home. Jalen then parks the car in the driveway, gets out, and walks to the front door. He then unlocks the front door and walks into the house. As soon as he walks in, his family is right there in the living room.

He immediately walks toward the stairs, looks over to his mom, and says. "I'm gonna take a shower; we did a whole bunch of stuff with the alarm system that was draining."

Lisa Collins looks at him and says."Okay, baby, you look drained too."

He walks up the stairs and takes his clothes off in his room, and groans in pain. Jalen then walks over to his dresser and gets his underclothes. He then proceeds to the bathroom and turns on the shower water, and he gets into the shower. Jalen then feels a lot better as the hot water starts to heal the bruises on his body.Jalen then gets out of the shower and says."Oh my gosh, I feel so much better now, I'm still a little sore, but I'm better now. My healing factor must have really kicked in." He then drys himself off and puts his underclothes on, and walks out of the bathroom into his room. Jalen then hangs his towel up behind his door, turns the tv on, and starts to get ready for bed. He lays down and eventually falls asleep.

Chapter 7

It's December 26th at nine-thirty in the morning, and Jalen wakes up in a great mood. He gets up and stretches in his room. He gets up and goes into the bathroom, and uses the bathroom. Jalen grabs his toothbrush, puts toothpaste on it, and starts brushing his teeth. After 5 minutes of brushing his teeth, he then starts washing his face with a face wash he uses. Afterward, he drys his face and moisturizes it with some shea butter, and goes downstairs to the kitchen.

Jalen stands there in the kitchen and questions himself." What should I eat for breakfast today?"

Jalen then walks over to the fridge and searches through the fridge to find something he's interested in eating.

Footsteps start approaching, walking down the steps, and Lisa Collins walks into the kitchen and says." Morning shugs, bear."

Jalen looks up and says to her. "Oh, what's up, ma."

Lisa Collins looks at him and asks." What are you looking for in the fridge?"

Jalen then says to her. "I'm looking for some food here, but we have nothing here to eat like always."

Jalen then laughs and shakes his head.

Lisa Collins then laughs at Jalen and says. "Yeah, I mean, it basically is every man for themselves up in here. If you were a coffee drinker, I'd tell you it's some coffee here."

He laughs and says." Trust me, ma, I've been figuring that out."

She says to him." We got cereal and oatmeal in here."

He walks over to the pantry and says." Oh, I guess we do have some food in here. I'm probably going to make some oatmeal, actually."

She starts walking away and says." Okay, well, I have to go ahead and get ready for work."

He then asks his mom." Aye, ma, his dad at work."

"Yeah, he left out at like 5 this morning; what's up?" she said to him and asked him.

He then replies and says." Oh, no reason, it's just I usually hear him when he's leaving out in the morning, but I guess I was completely knocked out."

Jalen then laughs, grabs the oatmeal packets out of the pantry, and grabs the loaf of the brioche bread. Jalen preps his oatmeal and makes some toast to go with it.

Bernard arrives at his office building two hours later, walks into his office room, and sits down at his computer. He then sits there and begins to feel bad for Jalen quitting. He then tries to call him, and it goes straight to voicemail, and he tries to call again. The phone goes to voicemail one more time. Bernard then looks down at the phone and says to himself." I guess he must not want to speak to me right now."

He gets up and puts Jalen's combat suit on the wall where it's supposed to go.

Bernard then says to himself." Hopefully, he changes his mind and comes back for it."

He sits down, starts working on some of his own projects, and puts the projects he worked with Jalen on away in the storage closet.

He then texts Jalen, saying." I was sorry for everything yesterday. I just want you to know I love you, and it's ultimately your decision if you're going to come back and help me."

Jalen finishes eating his oatmeal and toast. He then cleans his dishes, goes upstairs to his room, and relaxes there. Jalen looks down at his phone and sees that his Grandfather called him and texted him.

Jae locks his phone, puts it on the charger, and says aloud to himself." I really don't want to speak to Grandpa right now."

Jalen then closes his eyes, exhales, and lies on his bed facing the ceiling.

Jalen's phone rings, and Maya's name pops up. He then picks up the phone and says." Yo, what's up, Maya?"

Maya then says to him. "Hey Jae, what's up? What you got planned for the day?"

He smiles at her and says." Honestly, I literally have nothing planned for today."

Maya then asks Jalen." Well, do you think I can come over and hang out with you today?"He then exhales and says." Actually, not today I just want to relax in my bed today; I'm free tomorrow."

She laughs and says." Look, I understand entirely, Jae, so I will talk to you later."

Jalen then turns on his tv and says to her." Sounds cool; see you later, Maya."

Jalen grabs the remote and then flips through the channel, trying to find something to watch on TV. He then comes across an old cartoon show he used to love and sits there all day watching it in his room. He ends up falling asleep in his bed later that night.

Jalen wakes up in an excellent mood, gets out of his bed, and begins to do his morning stretches. He then starts his morning by doing his usual routine of using the bathroom and brushing his teeth. Afterward, he decides to take a shower.

Once he's done taking a shower, he says to himself. "Okay, let me see what Maya wants to do today because I have no idea what to do."

Jalen walks out of the bathroom, goes back into his room, and texts Maya saying." Okay, what's the move for today, baby girl?"

Jalen then sends the text and immediately regrets it and says to himself." Why would you say baby girl, you idiot?"

She then responds back almost immediately and says." I mean, it's whatever you want to do."

He smiles and looks at her through the phone and says." Say less if you want to I'm going to get some food from Rob's in a little while so let's start with some food."

She laughs at him and mentions to him. "Yo dude, you are fat, and yeah, that's perfect because I'm hungry."

He laughs at Maya and replies to her, saying." Oh wow, but yet you call me fat."

Maya smiles and says to him. "Yeah, you are fat because you always eating something, Jae."

He laughs and replies back to her. "I wasn't going to go over until rob said he wanted me to come over and try some new things for the menu."

She smirks at him and tells him." You know we should do a little eating contest between us."

Jae smiles at her and questions her." Wait, is this to a food contest, basically?"

"I sure did. Do I hear a bit of fear in your voice JalenCollins," Maya then says to him as she tries to intimidate him into a challenge?

"Damn, it's like that; you really want the smoke, huh?" he questions Maya's challenge.

"Yeah, I'm up for the challenge; go ahead and tell rob to set it up for us?" she then tells Jalen about her challenge and starts to laugh at him.

Jalen laughs and replies back to her. "Bet I'm going to call him right now and tell him then."

She laughs and tells him. "Okay, don't chicken out now because it's too late."

He then says to him." Ight I'll see you later. I'm going to call Rob right now."

She smiles at him and says." Okay, let me know what time we go there, and I will meet you there."

Jalen then hangs up and starts to call rob. Rob then picks up the phone and says. "What's up, little brother?"

He says to him. "Alright, so look, remember you wanted me to come over and test the new stuff for the menu."

"Yeah, why, what's up, Jae?" Rob asks him, kind of confused about what's going on.

Jalen then laughs and says to him. "Okay, so Maya wants to come, but she wants to turn it into a competition between us."

"Damn, Jae, she challenged you to an eating competition basically," rob said to his little brother.

He laughs and says to him." I know that junk crazy."

Rob laughs and says." So you want me to set everything up for y'all like a competition."

He snaps his finger and says," Yeah, precisely because she really thought I would punk out on this."

Rob looks at him and says." Hell Nah, I'm not about to let you chicken out on this one."

"Oh, Rob, I had no intentions of chickening out on this," he said.

Bernard goes back to the office and continues working on projects. Bernard starts to come up with a plan to stop Zion. He sits down at his computer and does some research. Bernard begins to look up the cloudburst and study how it works. As soon as Bernard starts figuring out how the machine will work.

He then says to himself." Oh geez, I need to get a drink real quick."

Bernard then gets up and walks over to the other side of his office and gets himself water. He then opens it up right before taking a sip of the water. An explosion goes off at the door of Bernard's office, and he gets blown back 15 feet in his office.

Bernard's office is in flames and smoke, and he starts coughing. Zion walks into the room with shaw and a couple of troops from his militia.

Zion then says out loud as he walks into the room. "Oops, I should have probably knocked on the door first."

Bernard coughs and says to himself. "Wait, I know that voice; it can't be."

Zion walks into the room and says." Hey Bernard, where are you."

Zion starts walking around his office looking for Bernard.

Shaw Drags Bernard to the middle of the office for Zion to see him. Bernard gets up and tries to hide behind some of the rubble. Shaw then finds Bernard hiding and grabs him. Zion then walks over to him and looks down at him.

Zion smiles at him and says. "It has been a long time, Bernard; you look, old man."

Zion looks at Bernard and laughs. He then finds a liquor bottle on the floor and picks it up. He then takes a sip and tosses the bottle across the room.

Bernard coughs and looks at him, and says. "Yeah, it has been a very long time, and it's been twenty-something years."

"I can't believe you gave your grandson the serum," Zion said to Bernard as he paced back and forth.

"The reason I gave him the serum has nothing to do with you," he said to Zion as he groaned in pain on the floor.

He looks at him and says. "Then you send him a child to try and stop me; that was a really bold move." He then paces in front of Bernard shaking his head in disgust.

He laughs and says to him." Yeah, but that kid is more brilliant and more robust than you ever could be."

He then laughs and says. "I'm not scared of a kid."

Bernard smiles and says. "I'm not saying be scared of him, but I'm telling you he will stop you."

Zion looks at him and says. "Okay, bump all of that enough about your grandson; where are the serums you stole from me."

Bernard looks up at him and says." Ahh, so that's what you came here for, huh."

"Yes, but I actually had other plans in store for with them," he said to Bernard as he bent down and looked him in the eye.

"You're talking about the cloudburst, aren't you?" Bernard asks Zion about his plans.

He then tells him." Yeah, I'm glad you listened to Jalen as he found intel and got his ass beat."

He then asks him as he lays on the floor in pain." What are you planning with serums, Zion?"

"Damn, I'm glad you actually asked about it; I redesigned the cloudburst into dispersing the mutation within the serum," he said about his plans.

Bernard looks up at him and says to him. "You're absolutely insane."

He looks down at him and replies to him saying. "I know I am, and when the clock strikes 12, everyone will know I'm insane."

Bernard then replies back to him. "I don't have the serums."

He looks at him and says." I know you have them because you stole about 8 vials of the serum from me."

He then looks at him and speaks to him. "I don't have those damn serums, okay? I destroyed them after I gave Jalen the serum."

He looks him dead in his face and says. "Do you think I'm an idiot? I know you're lying."

He looks at him and says. "What makes you think I'm lying?"

Zion laughs and punches him in the face and says." Listen, so if you keep lying, I will turn you into a punching bag until you talk."

He coughs up blood and says. "I'm not scared of you, Zion."

Zion picks him up by his throat, grabs his arm, and snaps it, breaking it.

Bernard screams in agony.

Zion then throws him across the room to where his desk is located. Bernard crashes into his desk, and 5 vials fall out of the desk and roll onto the floor.

Zion looks at the vials and says. "I knew you were lying to me."

The sirens start to approach the street, and Zion says to his henchmen." We need to leave now; we got what we came for."

Zion and his group exit the office and building.

Bernard lies between his broken desk, unconscious on top of broken wood.

Jalen gets to Rob's restaurant, gets out of the car, and walks inside. When Jae walks in, he sees rob setting up a table for him and Maya to do the little competition.

He walks over to his brother, daps him up, and says." Yo, what's up, bro."

Rob replies back to him and says." What's up, Lil bro."

"I haven't been doing anything but just chilling today," Jalen said to Rob as he helped set up.

He laughs and replies back to him." I feel you, man."

"Now, all I'm doing is just waiting for Maya to come now," he says to rob while looking at the door waiting for Maya.

Maya then walks in the door and looks around for Jalen. She then sees him, walks toward him, and hugs him.

She smiles at Jae, kisses him on the cheek, and says." Hey Rob, how are you."

He replies back to her and says. "What's up to? How are you doing?"

She responds back by saying. "I'm good, and I'm pretty sure your brother told you about the little competition we want to do."

He starts chuckling and says. "Yeah, he told me, that's why we're setting the table up right now."

"Yeah, honestly, I don't really care about the competition. I just want to eat. I'm hungry," Jalen said to both Rob and Maya.

"Yeah, I really didn't want to do a battle against you, I was just trying to come up with something, so I can eat some food too," she then responds to him about their one-on-one eating contest.

Rob looks at both of them and asks. "How about instead of a contest, let's just do a new menu tasting?"

Jalen looks over at rob and says. "Yeah, that's actually perfectly fine because that's what I was originally coming over for."

Maya looks at him and Rob and says. "Yeah, that's actually fine with me too."

Rob then looks at them and says." Bet I actually got a couple of things ready for y'all."

She then says while rubbing her stomach. "Yeah, please, I'm hungry, whatever you got."

Jalen puts his hand on his stomach and says." Bro, yes, I need food badly. I haven't eaten since like seven o'clock yesterday."

Rob then starts walking away as he laughs and says." Alright, I'll be right back."

Rob walks into the kitchen and grabs the fried rice and crab wontons. He then gets some homemade yum yum sauce he made from scratch. He puts the bowl of yum yum sauce onto the plate and takes it out to Jalen and Maya.

Jalen and Maya sit down at the table and talk when rob brings the food out.

Rob then says as he starts to set down the food on the table. "This is just some stuff to just start off with."

Maya smiles and says to him. "Thank you, rob this looks so good fr."

"Yo, is this the bacon fried rice?" Jalen then asks his brother as he looks at the rice.

He laughs at Jalen and then says to him. "Yeah, I figured you would like this because you haven't had it in such a long time."

"Yeah, I've been having a taste for this rice for a while now," he says to him as they start getting ready to eat their food.

Jalen and Maya sit together and enjoy their food as rob keeps bringing out food. Rob brings out multiple different egg rolls and other meats for the menu.

As they're sitting and eating, time passes, and Rob gets a phone call from their mom.

Lisa Collins picks up the phone. She then says." Robert, your Grandfather, is in the hospital."

Rob answers and asks his mother. "Wait, what happened, ma?"

Lisa then says to Rob over the phone. "There was some type of fire, and he was also found beaten pretty bad in his office. They took him in, and he's in surgery now."

Rob then responds back to Lisa. "Yeah, Jae and I are on our way, okay."

Rob then hangs up the phone and goes to tell Jalen what happened. Rob walks to the table and looks at Jalen.

Jalen looks at rob and asks him. "What's up, Rob? Why are you looking at me like that?"

He looks at him and says to him. "Grandpa is in the hospital, Jae."

He looks up at Rob and stops eating his food. He then says to him. "What happened to him, Rob?"

Maya looks up and asks the both of them. "Is everything okay with him?"

Rob looks at them and starts stacking their plates up. Rob then says to them. "We got to go. I told mom we would start making our way over there as soon as possible."

"Okay, let's go ahead and get going," Jae then says to them.

The three of them all get up from the table and walk out of the restaurant.

Jalen then says to them. "I'm going to drive by the way."

They all get in the car, and when Jalen grabs the steering wheel, he starts shaking. His nerves began to get really bad because he was worried about his Grandfather. He takes a deep breath and starts to drive to the hospital.

After minutes of driving down the road, they finally arrive at the hospital. They all get out of the car and enter through the emergency room entrance.

 Lisa is sitting there in the waiting lobby for them to come.

Jalen looks at his mom and says to her. "Hey ma, what happened exactly to him?"

Lisa looked at all three of them and said to them. "Jae is actually up right now and doing fine. He's just in a good amount of pain."

Rob looks at his mom and says to Lisa. "Okay, cool, so let's go see him."

Maya then smiles and says to them. "That's really good to hear he's doing okay."

They all begin to walk to the hospital room that Bernard is checked into. When they got to the room, Lisa opened the door slowly so, just in case Bernard was possibly sleeping. They all fully enter the room, and Bernard looks over at them.

They walk over to his hospital bed, and Bernard speaks to everyone as he groans in pain. "What's going on, everybody?"

Jalen looks down at him in the hospital bed and says to him. "What happened, Grandpa? We got over here as fast as possible?"

"Yeah, I appreciate it; you guys, it means a lot," Bernard looks up and says to everyone in the room.

They all look at Bernard, and Maya says to Bernard. "Of course, grandpa, we got to make sure you're okay."

He looks at Jalen as he grabs his hand and says to everyone in the room. "Hey everyone, can you guys give Jae and me a couple of minutes to talk about something?"

Everyone looks at Jae, and Lisa says to her dad Bernard. "Okay, we'll go look for your doctor and see when they will discharge you from the hospital."

Lisa, Rob, and Maya all walk out of the room to give Bernard and Jae space to talk. The door shuts, and Bernard starts to tell him about what happened. "Jalen, he's obtained everything he needs for the machine."

He looks at his grandpa, confused, and asks him. "Are you talking about Zion?"

He looks at him and replies back to Jalen. "Yes, Jae, we need to stop him because what he's planning will ruin lives and destroy the city."

Jalen looks at him and starts to walk away. Bernard then jumps up out of the hospital bed and grabs Jalen's arm, and looks at him with a face of desperation. Bernard looks at him and says to Jae. "Jae, I'm serious. I need you more than ever."

He looks him in the face and snatches his arm away. He then says to him in a frustrated tone. "I told you I'm done with this grandpa. What do you not get? I just want to be a kid?"

Bernard looks at him and says to him with a very unease tone. "Jae, you are the only person that can stop him and save the city. You have to be able to stop him by any means necessary."

"Are you telling me that I might have to kill Zion?" he simply asks his Grandfather.

He looks at him and nods his head, indicating yes.

He then looks at him and says to him. "Are you crazy? You're telling me to take his life. I'm not going to make that choice."

He looks at Jalen in his eyes and says back to Jae. "I need you, kid."

Jalen looks back at him with resentment and asks his Grandfather. "Why do you believe in me so much that I can beat him?"

Bernard tells him why he believes in him. "Well, first of all, you are my grandson, and I've never once seen you give up on anything in your life. It doesn't matter what the challenge is; you've found a way every time."

Jalen looks at him and says back to him. "Tell the cops about what you know and let them handle this. The hero gig is over for me."

Jalen walks away from the hospital bed and exits the room with anger.

Bernard holds his head down while lying in the hospital bed.

Jalen goes and finds Rob, Maya, and his mother and says to them. "Guys, I'm getting ready to leave."

Maya looks at him, confused about why he's leaving so soon, and replies to him saying. "Okay, you can drop me back off at home."

Rob looks over and says to his mom. "Well, my staff is holding it down while I'm here. I'll stay here with you, ma."

Lisa looked at rob and said to him. "Thank you because you know I hate hospitals, so it would be great if I'm not by myself."

"Yeah, no problem, ma. I actually needed a little break from the restaurant too. We were super busy within the last couple of days," Rob says to Lisa about him staying.

Jalen and Maya walk out of the emergency room and go to the car. Before she gets in the car, she looks at him and asks him. "Jae, is everything okay with you? You seem upset right now."

"Yeah, Maya, I'm actually okay, and I'm not upset about anything," he answers her right before they get in the car.

"Okay, I'm just making sure you know I have to check on you as well," she indicates to him as she opens her door to the car.

Jae gets in the car and turns it on. He then drives away and leaves the hospital. Jalen goes down the road for some time and then drops her off home. He then backs out of her driveway and drives to his Grandfather's office to see how bad the damage is to the building.

Jalen gets to the building and searches around, looking at the damage Zion caused to his Grandfather's office. He goes to where his suit and equipment are typically located and sees it's still there.

Jalen looks at the suit, smirks, and says aloud to himself. "Come on, Jalen, what are you doing here? You know don't really want to be here."

Jalen walks over to the training room entrance and walks down the stairs. Jalen then walks into the room and sits down, looking around at all of the stuff in the room. He then stands up and exhales very slowly.

Jalen has a hard time thinking about if he should come back to help his Grandfather stop Zion or not. Jalen then leaves the office, drives home, and goes into his room. Jalen spends the rest of the night wondering if he could actually make a difference or would he just fail the city and his Grandfather. Jalen looks up at the ceiling and just stares into space. He then sits and thinks about his future with this and basketball. He sits and wonders on choosing this path of being a hero, or vigilante will change him and make him into someone he's not. He contemplates what Bernard said about him having to possibly take Zion's life.

He then says to himself. "There's another way I won't just settle for that."

Jae sits up in his bed and thinks about different non-lethal ways to neutralize Zion. He then falls asleep.

The following day he wakes up and goes to the hospital. When Jalen gets to the hospital, he goes to the room that Bernard was checked into. He opens the door and sits down in front of the bed that Bernard is sleeping in.

Bernard sees him sitting in the chair and as starts to wake up. He then asks Jae. "Let me guess, you've made your decision, huh?"

He looks at him and says back. "Yeah, I have grandpa, actually."

After hearing him say that, he smirks at him and asks him. "Okay, so what did you decide to do?"

Jae looks at him and exhales. Jae then says to his Grandfather. "I'm going to try and stop him in a non-lethal way."

"He's a monster that needs to be stopped. Being non-lethal is not how we should do this," he says to Jalen.

Jalen looks at him and says back to Bernard. "Grandpa, there is no we. I was the one out there that got their ass kicked last time I checked. And where were you?"

Bernard looks at Jalen and replies back. "I know, Jae, I wasn't there when you needed me to be there."

Jae looks at his Grandfather with anger and says to him. "Exactly, that's what I mean. I'm the one out there wearing that suit, so don't tell me about making the decision on whether he lives or dies. If you come back on this crusade, it will be by my rules."

He sits up in the hospital bed and says. "What don't you understand, son? Is this the only way to stop him?"

He looks up at the ceiling and says. "Grandpa, you literally told me yesterday you believed in me because I never give up. The decision you're making is giving up and choosing to give up, and that's not what I'm going to do ever. You need me just as much as I need you, and the only way that works is if we come to an agreement."

He walks out of the hospital room and leaves. Jalen gets in his car and punches the steering wheel.

He says to himself. "You stubborn old man."

He turns on his car and drives away, leaving the hospital. He then moves down the road to Maya's house. When Jalen arrives at Maya's home, he gets out of his car and walks ups to her front porch.

He then rings her doorbell, and Maya answers the door, and she says to Jalen. "Jae, what are you doing here?"

He then says to her. "I don't know. I was in the area, and I was just like, let me see what she's doing now."

She looks at him, confused, and tells him. "Okay, cool if you want to go out and get some hot chocolate or just chill in the house?"

He looks at her and says. "Yeah, we could just make some hot chocolate and chill in the house."

"Okay, come on in. I know it's cold out there," Maya then says to him as she opens the door more for him to walk inside her home.

The two of them start laughing, and he walks in the door. He goes and sits down on the couch.

Maya looks at Jae and tells him. "Hold on, I'll be right back. I'm going to go get my phone out of my room."

Maya walks upstairs and grabs her phone out of the room, and comes back downstairs.

The two make hot chocolate, go into the kitchen, and make pancakes to enjoy their hot chocolate. The two of them sit down and watch movies for the rest of the day on the couch. They snuggle together under blankets laughing and enjoying each other's company.

Hours pass by, and he tells her. "Okay, Maya, this has been a fun and chill day, but I have to go."

She looks at him as there sitting on the couch and says. "Dang, do you really need to?"

Jalen takes the blanket off of himself and says. "Yeah, I'm getting a little tired, so I'm going home and sleeping."

She looks at him and says. "Okay, I completely understand; go ahead and go. Just let me know when you get home."

Maya walks Jaleen to the door. Maya grabs him before walking off the porch and gives him a kiss. They stop kissing and smile at each other. He walks away and gets in his car. Jalen starts his car and drives out to go home.

When he arrives, he goes straight to his room, takes his clothes off, and goes to the bathroom. Jalen then takes a shower, and afterward, he gets in his bed and goes to sleep.

The following day on December 29th, Jalen wakes up to a call from his Grandfather. Jalen picks up the phone.

He says to him. "I need you to meet me at the office, Jae."

Jalen then says to him over the phone. "Okay, Grandpa, see you in an hour."

An hour passes by. Jalen gets to the office and walks inside Bernard's office room. He walks into the room. Bernard is standing in the middle of the room with his left arm in a cast.

Jalen says to him. "You wanted to see me, grandpa?"

He sighs and looks and Jae and says. "Jae, I was wrong, and I'm sorry that I didn't realize that until now."

He crosses his arms and questions him saying. "What is it exactly that you're wrong about?"

"I was wrong when I told you that you have to kill him to stop, which is not true," he then tells him why he's apologizing.

Jalen looks at him and says. "Well, I'm glad you actually realized it."

He looks at him and says. "Jae, I need you, though, because he will succeed in his plan without you."

Jalen uncrosses his arms and sighs.

"Grandpa, I told you the only way I'm coming back is if you let me do this my way," he said to his grandpa as he began to accept his apology.

Bernard looks Jalen in the eye and says to him. "Okay, I'm going to let you run this whole thing because, like you said, you are the one that's out there in the suit, not me."

Jalen smirks and tells him. "I'm in; just remember that I call the shots on this."

The two of them shake hands and smile. Bernard then says to Jalen. "Well, let's get to it then."

He smiles and then says. "Okay, so what happened when Zion came here, Grandpa. Walk me through everything that happened."

Bernard tells him. "He came looking for the serums I stole from him years ago."

Jalen looks at him, confused, and questions him. "What does he want with the serums, grandpa?"

Bernard looks at him and sighs, and tells him. "He needs it to complete the machine."

"Wait, why does he need the serums, though, grandpa?" Jae then asks his Grandfather again, still confused.

Bernard sighs and tells him why. "Jae, it was his plan, along with serums and the cloudburst. "

Jalen looks at him and says. "The serum is the compound he's planning to release in the cloudburst?"

Bernard looks at him and nods his head. Jalen looks at him and says. "Damn, of course, he would be planning that. That's why he said he trying to help mankind evolve."

Jae then starts pacing slowly in the office room.

"Do you know what his timeframe is, though?" He then asks his Grandfather.

Bernard says to him. "No, I do not know when he's planning on doing this. The only thing he said was when the clock strikes 12, everyone will know he's insane."

Jalen looks at him and says. "What does that even mean? When the clock strikes 12, what is he referring to?"

He paces around the room once more and sighs. He then realizes and says to himself. "New Year's Eve that's when he planning his attack on the city Grandpa."

Bernard looks at him and says. "Damn, how did I not see that."

Jalen looks at him and says. "We need to find out where he's planning it to go off."

Bernard looks at Jae and says. "We have to figure out how to stop that machine because once it goes off, every person in this city's life will forever change."

Jalen then says to him. "Let's get to work."

Jalen and Bernard start moving all of the equipment to the training room. The two of them start prepping to build more gadgets and technology for them to stop Zion. Jalen begins to create designs for a new dart holster and makes new types of darts. Bernard starts making upgrades to the suit.

They both spend the rest of the day planning and creating tech for them to stop the cloudburst. The two of them sit there and look through some research to find out how the cloudburst works and how they could destroy it.

Maya walks into the office room where Jalen and Bernard are standing therein.

She looks at them and says. "Wow, so this is where you have been all winter break?"

Jalen turns around immediately with a pen in his mouth and safety goggles. He then looks and says to her. "What are you doing here?"

She sighs and replies to Jae saying. "Well, I went over to your house, and your mom said you weren't there, and the only other place I knew I would find you would be here."

Jalen sighs.

"You shouldn't be Maya; it's too dangerous," he said to her.

She looks at him and says. "Wait, what, why?"

He looks at her and says. "It just is okay. I can't explain it."

She then looks at Jalen and walks into the room over to Jalen. She says to him. "Tell me what's going on here. What's all of this right here?"

Jalen looks at her and says. "It's nothing to worry about, Maya."

Bernard looks at him and says. "Just tell her Jae it's okay. I trust her."

He replies to him. "You told me not to tell anybody."

He responds back to him by saying. "Yeah, but I trust Maya too because she loves you, and you feel the same way back."

"What is it tell me?" She then asks Jae as they stand there in the middle of the room.

Jalen looks at her and sighs. He then tells her. "Okay, when we got attacked at the mall. I put on a suit that gave a perilous person my location that needed to get to my Grandfather. He needed to get these serums to turn a normal person into an abnormal, creating living weapons. I also found out recently that I have that same serum running through my blood. This dangerous man's name is

Zion, and he plans to disperse this serum over the city on New Year's Eve at 12. It's my job to stop because nobody else can go hand to hand with him."

Maya looks at him with a face of shock and says. "Wait to hold on; you mean to tell me that you basically have superpowers and you have to fight a supervillain?"

He looks at her and chuckles, and says. "Yeah, basically when you put it that way."

Maya looks at him with anger and says. "So you lied when you told me that the police were going to handle the situation at the mall? Jalen, this is crazy; how are you so calm about this?"

Jalen sighs and rolls his eye at her, and says to her. "I lied to protect you, actually, Maya. Honestly, I don't know how I've been so calm about it, but I guess it's because I've always felt different from everyone else."

Maya says to him. "I'm not going to tell any, of course."

Bernard looks at her and says. "Do you want to come over here and be an extra set of hands because we need all the help we could get?"

Maya looks at both of them and says. "Yeah, I could help."

Jalen pulls Maya to him closely and hugs her. He then says to her. "Don't worry, I won't ever let anything happen to you." Jae then kisses Maya on her forehead.

Maya looks up at him and says. "You could have told me, Jae; you know any secret is safe with me."

"I know I just didn't want to put you in any danger, and grandpa told me not to tell anyone," he says to her.

She looks at Jalen's Grandfather and says. "Grandpa, what is the plan to find this Zion guy."

He responds back to her by saying. "We're trying to figure that out right now; so far, we know it will happen on New Year's Eve. Zion doesn't want to be discreet about this; he wants everyone to see his big plan."

Jalen looks at him and questions him. "Well, how do you know that, grandpa?"

Bernard looks at him and says. "I know because that's who he is."

She looks over at Jalen and says. "Well, I was going to invite you to go with my family and me to the plaza."

Jalen chuckles and then stares off into space and finally realizes something. He then says to both Maya and Bernard. "Okay, if I'm looking for attention, especially on New Year's Eve, where would they go?"

Maya looks at him and says. "You would go to the city plaza."

Jalen looks at her and says. "Exactly, it's right in the middle of the city."

Bernard looks at him, pulls up the city plaza map, and sighs.

Jalen and Maya look at the map of the city plaza, and he says to them. "He's going to have the machine go off in the Plaza. Not out in the open but in one of these buildings in the Plaza. The Plaza is where thousands of people in the city plan on being on that night, so that's it. The only thing is how to find him because he's going to be right next to the machine. He won't risk any chances of it being shut down, so he's going to right next to it."

She looks at him and shakes her head.

Bernard looks at Jalen and says. "If I try to locate the cloudburst machine by singling out the energy signature. A machine like that will produce a tremendous amount of energy and power."

He then tells his grandpa. "Grandpa, the second you find the machine is the same as we find Zion, we stop him."

The next day Jalen wakes up at home and checks his phone for missed calls or messages. He looks at the date and time and sees that its December 30th and 10 o'clock in the morning. Jalen gets up and does his regular morning routine. He then goes downstairs and makes himself a bowl of cereal. After finishing his cereal, he goes upstairs and puts his clothes on. Jalen then leaves the house and gets in the car to go to his Grandfather's office.

Time passes, and he finally arrives at his Grandfather's office. He parks his car and gets out. Jalen then heads inside to see Bernard.

He knocks on Bernard's door and asks him when he will get inside. "What's going on, grandpa?"

Bernard looks at him and says. "You need to do some training exercises, and I'm going to work on some upgrades to your gear."

He looks at him and sighs and responds, saying. "I'm not going to lie; I figured that's what was going to happen."

He chuckles and says to him. "Things will be a little different this time because I made some modifications to the training dummies."

Jalen takes his shirt off and starts to puts his suit on. He then asks him. "What new things did you add to it, grandpa ?"

He smirks and says. "Yeah, I added different types of fighting styles to it. It's going to make you a better fighter. I know it will take some time, but today I want you to just train all day."

Jalen then goes to the training area, does some stretches, and says. "Hey, grandpa, I think I might be a little rusty because it has been a couple days."

Bernard laughs at him and says. "Hell no, because Zion won't take it easy on you. Just stay focused and remember all of your training so far."

Jalen looks at him from the training room and smirks. He then says. "Okay, grandpa, you got a valid point right there."

Jalen gets into his fighting stance, and Bernard activates the dummies. Jalen spends the next couple of hours pushing himself to the limit. He starts to sweat excessively due to his long training sessions.

Maya arrives and walks in. She looks at Jalen training and smiles at him, admiring him.

Maya then says to both of them. "I brought food for everyone if you guys are hungry."

He stops training and says. "Okay, I'm starving because I've been training for hours."

Jalen then grabs a towel and wipes the sweat from his face and head. Maya walks up to him and tries to hug him.

Jalen looks at her and says. "I wouldn't get too close to me because I have been sweating a lot."

Maya laughs at him and says. "Yeah, it's all good. I don't mind."

Bernard gets up from his desk and goes and gets some of the food that Maya brought for him.

The three of them sit there and enjoy the rest of their night, eating food, laughing, and talking.

An hour later, Zion starts to prepare everything for tomorrow to fulfill his plan. Shaw starts moving the machine into a truck, and the militia begins to leave out.

Zion then looks over at Shaw and says. "Nothing will get in my way. I will succeed by any means necessary."

Shaw looks at him and asks him. "What do you need me to do, Sir?"

Zion starts walking away and says. "I need you to protect the building with your life because I will not let Bernard and his grandson ruin my plan."

Chapter 8

The next day on the 31st, Jalen wakes up in his room and contemplates what will happen later. Jalen then goes downstairs and sees his mother in the kitchen.

He then walks over to her and says. "Hey, what's up, ma?"

Lisa turned around, surprised to see Jalen as she was making her coffee, and said to him. "Hey, what's up with you?"

Jalen looks at her and says. "Nothing, I was just getting ready to head out to Grandpa and help him clean up his office. What do you and dad have planned for tonight?"

Lisa looked at him and said. "That's nice that you're going to help him clean, and honestly, I didn't think we're going to do anything."

Jalen sighs in relief and says to her. "Okay, good."

Lisa took a sip of her coffee and said. "That is some good coffee. What made you even ask me about our plans tonight?"

Jalen looks at her and says."Oh, no reason. I was just asking because Maya wanted me to go with her and her family to the plaza to watch the countdown. I just wanted to make sure you didn't have anything planned for us."

Lisa smiled and said. "Oh yeah, go ahead and have fun. I will probably be in the house cooking tonight because I already went to the store yesterday."

He looks at her and says. "Okay, ma, that sounds good to me."

He then goes upstairs and starts getting ready to head over to his grandfather's building. Jalen spends the next 20 minutes getting dressed. Afterward, Jalen walks downstairs, goes out the door, and gets in his car. Jalen backs out of his driveway and remembers that he has to pick up

Maya. Jalen drives over to her house. Ten to fifteen minutes pass by, arriving at Maya's house.

He then texts her and says. "Hey, I'm outside."

She then responds to him and says. "Okay, cool, I'm coming out right now, Jae."

Jalen then sits in his car, listening to music while waiting for her to come out. She then comes out of the house and locks her door. She then walks off her front porch, starts making her way to his car, and gets in it.

When she gets in the car, she looks over at him, smiles, and says. "What's up, Jae? How are you feeling today?"

He looks at her and says. "Honestly, to tell you the truth, I don't know how to feel right now. I don't know if I should be scared or worried that I can't beat him and stop that machine."

She gazes into Jalen's eyes, grabs his face, and says to him. "Jae, you're going to beat him and stop that machine because you are one of the strongest people I've ever met. Not to forget that you are also one of the bravest people I've ever met."

Jalen smiles at her and kisses her on her forehead. As a sign of showing thanks for the pep talk.

He then puts the car in reverse and backs out of the driveway. The two of them head over to Bernard's office. When they get to the building, they get out of the car and walk inside. They enter the room and see Bernard working on some stuff wearing his lab coat and safety goggles.

Jalen walks up to Bernard and says. "Grandpa, how long have you been at it?"

He looks over at him and says to Jae. "What do you mean, Jae?"

Jalen looks and him and sighs, and says. "How long have you been up working on things, Grandpa?"

Bernard looks at Jae and Maya as he takes his safety goggles off and says to Jae. "I've been up since like five o'clock this morning working these upgrades for you."

Maya sighs and says. "Grandpa, you need to take a nap."

Jalen looks at Maya and tells his grandfather. "Yeah, Grandpa, I agree with her because it's gonna be a long night, so please take a quick nap."

He looks at both of them and says. "Yeah, you guys are right. I've just been trying to ensure that you're fully equipped."

Jalen looks at him and says. "Yeah, I know, Grandpa, that's why I was going to start making the new darts and a wrist shooter. I need your help when you wake back up because I'm making a utility belt to hold my dart ammo on it and other gadgets."

Bernard looks at him, surprised, and says. "Dang, what made you even think about making that?"

Jalen looks at him and smiles, and says. "I mean, I will need a place to store my equipment on myself, so I said why not."

She smirks at Jalen and says. "Okay, now see, that's really cool."

Bernard looks at him and smirks, and says. "I like it too, Jae; just show me the blueprint when I wake up from this nap. Oh, is there any way you guys could get some food up here because I'll probably wake up super hungry?" Bernard then lays down on a bed in the nanotech training room.

Jalen then walks over to the computer in the lab and pulls up the design for the new dart he made with nanotech materials. He grabs a lab coat and safety goggles and starts crafting his new weapons.

Jalen realizes that Maya is just sitting there and decides to ask her. "Maya, would you like to help me out with this?"

Maya smiles at him and says. "Yeah, because you're going to need all the help you can possibly get."

Maya then goes and grabs a lab coat and some safety goggles. She walks over to where he is, and they smile at each other. He then diagnostics on the old design to darts and notices they're too skinny. Jalen makes them thicker and with a rubber tip of the dart to make it non-lethal.

Jalen starts to create the rubber tip for over a hundred darts and designs multiple different kinds of darts. He makes an explosive dart with a rubber tip and gun powder in the barrier of the dart that's supposed to ignite when the rubber head is hit with enough force. A knock dart that explodes tear gas out of the rubber head because that broad-head is designed to pop on impact. He also made a split dart that burst open with a rope to tie enemies up.

She looks at Jalen and says. "This is one of the coolest days of my life."

He laughs and says to her. "I know this is pretty crazy, right."

She looks at Jae and says. "Actually, I think this rated as number one on the coolest days I have ever had."

Jalen laughs at her and says. "I'm going to work on this new idea with the utility belt."

He goes over to the computer and finishes up his design for the belt. To soon start crafting it, but before he does, he remembers that he needs to create a case to hold his extra dart on him.

A couple of hours pass, and Zion arrives with his militia in the city's heart at the plaza. They park the trucks in the back of the building where the city will administrate the New Year's Eve countdown. They try to load the cloudburst into the building quietly, but a Security guard comes outside to take a smoke break. He then sees a small army on the landing dock of the building.

He grabs his radio and tells his fellow guards.

When shaw appears behind him and coves his mouth and says. "I think you should have just minded your business because now that cost you your life!"

Shaw then stabs him, and the security guard falls straight to the ground with a stab wound in the middle of his abdomen.

Zion walks up to Shaw and says. "Wonderful Shaw, that's what I want you to do. Guard this building with your life. Anyone that gets in my way makes them pay. Do you hear me?"

Shaw then scrambles the radio frequency and disables the camera to make them from security to cause them no problems as they bring the cloudburst in.

Shaw looks up at Zion and says. "Yes, sir, I will not let you down again!"

Zion looks over at the part of the militia that unloads the cloudburst and tells them. "Hurry up and get it inside the building."

Zion walks into the building with Shaw by his side. Zion and his army start assembling the cloudburst. Zion's army brings in the machine to set it up. The cloudburst is disassembled in crates, and they load it up to the top floor on the three main elevators.

Zion then walks over to the window and says to Shaw. "Shaw, I need you to take some of these men down to the main two floors so we can stop anybody that comes in. Oh, shaw also takes out all of the security guards in the building. We have to maintain control of this building."

Shaw looks at Zion and says to him. "Yeah, I will. I will take Twenty-five of our men, and we will monitor the two ground floors."

Zion looks at him and says. "Okay, once the rest of them are done up here putting the machine together, I'll send the rest of them down to you."

Shaw nods his head and walks downstairs with his troops. Shaw then goes to the main security room and knocks out all the guards.

A couple of hours pass. Bernard wakes up in the office and goes over to where Jalen was standing in the lab.

Bernard pats him on the back and says. "Jae, I like the designs for the new darts, and I'm going to a look at the utility belt."

Jalen looks at him and says. "Yeah, I can pull it up on the screen and show it. If you like what you see, we could start on it for sure."

Jalen puts his ammo carts in the open slot compartments. He then pulls up the blueprints for the utility belt for Bernard to see. Bernard looks and inspects the belt and makes some adjustments, and they agree on it. Jalen looks at Bernard, and they start crafting the belt. They make the belt reinforced with titanium and with detachable magnetic slots.

Jalen looks over at Maya and says. "Maya, tell your parent to stay away from the plaza tonight. I don't want anything to happen just in case, okay."

She looks at him and says. "Yeah, I know I told them hopefully, they don't go actually."

Bernard tells them both. "You guys need to make sure that no one you know goes to the plaza tonight because I'm pretty sure Zion is not going down without a fight."

Jalen then says. "Yeah, I asked my mom, and she said she gonna stay in the house and just cook."

Barnard looks at the time on the computer and sees that it's 10:45 pm. He then finally shows Jalen the new suit he made for him. The suit is all black with emerald green trimming. The radar goes off, indicating the machine was turned on. Jalen goes over to the new suit, puts it on, puts on his utility belt, and puts his wrist gauntlets on.

He says to his Grandpa. "Okay, grandpa, what building is he in so I know before I leave here."

Bernard looks at him and says. "He's in whatever building is smack dab in the middle of the plaza. I just checked the satellite, and it's about 3 thousand people in the plaza right now as we speak."

Jalen looks at him and says. "So I guess it's gone time then this is it."

Jae starts to walk over to the stairs to leave out. Maya grabs his arm before he goes up the stairs.

She then tells him. "You better come back to me because I can't lose you!"

He looks at her and tells her. "I promise you, Maya, I will return to you."

Jae then gazes into her eyes, immensely kisses her passionately, and walks up the stairs to leave the building. Jae then begins to make his way to the plaza and jumps from rooftop to rooftop.

Zion stands at the window and says. "Look at everyone standing in the plaza. They don't even know I'm about to change their lives forever. Rewarding them all with amazing gifts."

He gets to the building and says into his com-link. "Okay, grandpa, I'm here."

Bernard looks through Jalen's mask and says to him. "Okay, I installed a new thing to your lens; it's a thermal vision that will show every person in the building."

Jalen taps his lens and puts the thermal vision on, and sees everyone from the bottom floor to the top floor.

Jalen looks around the whole building and says."Okay, I can see everyone in the building. This thermal vision is incredible; Grandpa and I can see thirty-one people on the first two floors and one person on the top floor. I just need to figure out where to enter the building from."

Bernard tells him."Take a peek at the back entrance of the building, and if it's clear, go in there. You have to take out everyone on the ground floor, then move to Zion because I know he's up there with the cloudburst."

Jalen looks down at the crowd in the plaza and starts to make his way to the back entrance by jumping from building to building. He then zooms in on his lens and sees entirely clearly. He then repels down the building to make his way inside. He then goes inside the building, sees some of

Zion's troops in the hallway, and takes them out quickly and quietly.

Jalen finds the security room and takes out the three soldiers in the room. Jalen turns the cameras on and unblocks the radio frequency of the building. Jalen then starts to make his way to the main lobby, where another soldier stands in the walkway to the main entrance. Jalen then shoots his new knockout dart at the ground next to the soldier, and he smells the gas and immediately passes out. Right before he hits the floor, Jalen catches him to avoid him from falling and making a loud noise.

Jae then says to Bernard on the com-link. "Okay, grandpa, I'm here on the ground floor, and there's a lot of them down here too."

Bernard tells him. "Go ahead and test out those new darts, Jae."

Jalen laughs and says."Yeah, I think it's the perfect time for that, but I wonder which one I should start with."

Jalen peaks into the lobby room and looks at all the soldiers protecting the ground floor. He then puts his wrist shooter into battle mode. The battle mode on the wrist shooters increases the ammo capacity from 12 darts on each wrist shooter to 25. Jalen grabs two ammo clips for his darts. Jalen's suit absorbs the ammo cartridge, and the wrist shooter's nanotech starts to form and puts the rest of the darts onto his forearm. He then switches his dart to explosive darts. Jalen then aims at three guards, and they all get blown back. They all get knocked unconscious from the blast of the explosion.

Jalen then switches his dart on shuffle mode causing him to all of the darts at free will.

Shaw then hears an explosion and looks over and sees smoke located where Jalen fired his dart at the three soldiers down unconscious.

Shaw tells all the soldiers that are still conscious."Stay on your toes, men; we have an intruder here."

Shaw then tells Zion over a walkie-talkie. "I think he's here, boss."

Zion smiles as he stares out the window and speaks back into the walkie-talkie. "Well, be sure to give him a warm welcome."

Jalen then slides into the lobby from a hallway and completely opens fires shooting darts everywhere. Five of the soldiers rush towards Jalen as he stands in the middle of the lobby floor. He then starts to fight each soldier one by one. One of them tries to strike Jalen, and he dodges it. Jae roadhouse kicks the guy in the rib cage and then hits him with a right overhead hook to the face knocking the guy out completely. He then looks at the other guys coming at him and says.

"Come on, show what you guys got," Jae says to the enemies as they go down so easy.

Jae then performs a series of attacks on the goons that run at him. Jae's legs sweep one of them and punch him as soon as he falls down, knocking him out. He hits the next one with a front kick to the midsection and then uppercuts him right in the chin. The guy goes like ten feet flying backward from the uppercut that Jalen struck him with.

Jalen then hits the next one with a flying knee to the face, and he then shoots an explosive dart at him. The guy then goes flying back into the pillar located in the lobby. Jalen then starts shooting his darts at the rest of the men. He takes out about twenty men in the hall, leaving him to go one-on-one with Shaw.

Shaw then walks up to where Jalen is and draws his sword. The two of them face-off off each other, having a stand-off.

Shaw then says to him. "Jalen, I'm letting you know that this will be quick, so come on. You're not going to get upstairs to Zion."

He laughs at him and says. "Bonehead, I will get past you; let us go ahead and get this over with."

He then shoots a dart at Shaw, and he dodges it. Shaw then rushes toward Jalen with his sword and tries to slash at Jalen. Jalen then dodges his attack and counters with a roundhouse kick with his right leg to Shaw's abdomen. Shaw coughs from the pain of the kick. Shaw then elbows Jalen in the stomach. Jalen then hunches over from that blow, and Shaw then uppercuts Jae. Jalen stumbles back a couple of feet from the uppercut. Shaw then tries to stab Jalen, and he dodges his attack. Jae then knocks the sword out of Shaw's hand with a kick to his arm. After that, the two of them spend minutes trading blows, going back and forth. Jalen then does a double backflip to create space between him and shaw. He then switches his darts to explosive and shoots the dart at shaw, causing him to go flying out the building into the street where people are standing in the plaza crowd. People start panicking in the plaza, screaming and running away from the building. Jalen then falls down to the floor and sighs.

Jalen then says to himself as he tries to catch his breath. "Damn, that took a lot longer than I thought."

Bernard says to him while he's looking at the clock. "Jalen, you need to get a move on; you have thirty minutes left!"

Jalen then goes to the elevator and pushes the button to call for the elevator. It then explodes, sending Jalen flying back like 20 feet in the lobby. He then gets up, coughing and groans in pain from the explosion.Bernard looks at his lens to see what going on and sees smoke and fire.

Bernard then says to Jalen. "Jalen, you need to get up and stop that machine! You got twenty-five minutes, kid!"

Maya then says to Grandpa. "Dang, it, Grandpa, turn on channel 6. The building is on the news; they reported multiple explosions. They have the cops on the way to the building."

Bernard then turns the tv to the news and sighs. He starts to hack into the location of where the cops are at.

He then says to him. "Look, Jae, you three minutes to get Zion because the police will have the building surrounded, and they will breach the lobby."

Jalen then gets up and looks around and sees that the lobby is on fire and smoking. He sees that the stairs are blocked as well. He then walks outside and looks up at the building.

He then says to Bernard. "Okay, grandpa, I have to climb up the building because the stairs and elevator are both out of commission."

Bernard tells him. "Okay, hurry up and go for it because they'll be there at any moment."

Jalen shoots his grappling dart in front of the crowd of the people in the group.

Maya at the tv and said to Jalen. "Jae, they have you on the news; they just saw you fire your dart up the building."

The dart connects to the top of the building. Jalen retracts the grappling cable to go up the building. He then gets on top of the building. Tries to figure out a way to the floor where Zion and the machine are located. He then looks at his thermal vision.

He says to himself. "Okay, this is going to be really risky."

Jae then walks to the side of the building that Zion is closer to and shoots a grappling dart to the roof of the building. Jalen then jumps off the building and shoots an explosive dart at the window that Zion is standing next to. Zion gets blown back from the window. Jalen then jumps through the window. Zion then gets up and does a back handspring creating space between him and Jalen. They look each other at and begin to have a stand-off. Jalen then aims his wrist darts at Zion and moves away from the window. He then looks over at the cloudburst.

Zion looks over at him and says to him, yelling. "I won't let you get in the way of my plan! I'm doing this to change lives!"

Jalen looks at him and says. "Yeah, you're going to destroy lives; you have no idea the effect of this machine."

Zion chuckles as he stands with his hands behind his back and says. "Child, you nor your grandfather will ever understand my reasons behind this."

Jalen looks at him and says. "Yeah, I know this has something to do about your younger brother that died years ago but don't make everyone pay for what happened to him."

Zion then says to Jalen in a nonchalant tone. "That actually has a part of why I'm doing this. The real reason is to give to the poor. The minorities need the power to fight back against the oppressors of their society."

Jalen then says to him. "Dude, you're insane! Who are you to play god or even be a judge to the system?"

Zion then says to him. "I'm not playing god; all I'm doing is giving people the power to take down the corruption in this world."

Jalen then says to him angrily. "You don't get it. You could potentially give the wrong tools to a terrorist or serial killer. These powers could fall in the hands of someone with dangerous intentions."

Zion looks at Jalen, confused at what he says, and replies back to him. "Welp, I don't know what to tell you."

Bernard looks at Jalen's lens camera and tells him. "Jalen, he stalling you until the machine is ready."

Jalen chuckles and says out loud. "How did I not notice that man?"

Bernard sighs, and Maya says to Jalen. "Jalen, take him out and stop the machine."

Jalen then aims the darts at him and fires at Zion. Zion then dodges the darts fired at him by doing a series of backflips. After Zion lands the last backflip, he then throws a barrage of small knives at Jalen. Jalen then does a side flip to maneuver out the way of the blades. Jalen lands on his feet and shoots more darts at Zion.

Zion dodges the darts again, and small explosions go off behind him. The window crash open, and glass shatters all over the place. Tiny glass shards fall down the building. Cause injuries to people in the crowd. The channel 6 news helicopter flies up to the top floor of the building. Zion does a front-flip to Jalen and kicks him in the face.

Jalen then stumbles back and drops to one knee, and shoots another explosive dart at Zion at almost point-blank range. He then goes flying around through the wall twenty feet behind him.

Jalen then goes over to the machine and asks his Grandpa. "How do I deactivate it?"

Bernard looks and says. "You have to drain the power from it somehow or remove the core. Whatever the energy source is, remove it from the machine."

Jalen looks around, searching for the core or power source of it. He then realizes that it runs on ordinary electricity. It's plugged into all the outlets on the current floor thereon. He then says to Bernard. "Grandpa, the cloudburst is running on regular electricity."

Zion then gets up from the wall's rubble that collapsed on him. He then rushes toward Jalen with a burst of rage and screams at him saying. "You will not ruin my plan."

Zion lunges at Jalen and tackles him, and starts attacking him. He starts punching him in his ribs and his face. Jalen then counters one of his punches and elbows him in the chin. He then pushes him off and gets up off the floor. Jalen then gets up, and Zion gets up as well. The two of them face each other and get ready to fight one last time.

The new helicopter finally reaches the floor they're located on and shines the light on the two of them fighting, and its broadcasted live to the news.

Jalen then lands a series of blows on Zion, and he then roadhouse kicks Zion in the face. Zion then hits a four-punch combo and uppercuts Jalen's chin. He then groans on the floor and coughs from the pain.

Zion then looks at him and says. "You're not going to ruin this for me! Do you hear me?"

Jalen looks at Zion and says to him. "Dude, you're literally about to ruin people's lives forever."

Zion then walks over to the machine, presses the button to activate the device, and says to Jalen. "No, I'm changing lives for the better starting now."

The machine then activates and pulses. Zion then says to him. "Now that I started the machine, it's only a matter of time until the serum is in the troposphere and when it rains. The rain will mask the serum, and everyone in this city will have the same thing running through their veins as you and me."

The machine then sends energy surges to the roof, and electrical currents run over the top. The news helicopter then starts to film the energy surge on the roof.

Jalen then looks at Zion and says to him. "What have you done, Zion?"

Zion laughs at him and says to him. "Happy new year's, and I did what was necessary."

Jalen then limbs over to Zion, and he then grabs Jalen and tries to pick him up. He then struggles against him and fires more explosive darts, breaking all the windows. He then picks Zion up and slams him to the floor. Zion then groans in pain from the slam directed to his back.

Zion looks at him and says. "It's already over; Jalen, the machine has already been activated; you can't stop it." Zion then laughs manically at Jalen.

Jalen then walks over to the machine and asks his grandfather. "Okay, what should I do now that it's been activated."

Bernard then says to Jalen as he starts fidgeting in his chair back at the office building. "Jae, try unplugging every cord first, and if that doesn't work, you have to destroy the machine. That's the only thing I could think of, honestly."

Jalen then goes over to Zion and says. "How do you turn it off, Zion?"

Zion chuckles while lying on the floor and says. "You can't; it's already started. The only way is to destroy it."

Jalen then looks at him, punches him, knocks him out, and says. "Well, that's what I will have to do."

Jalen then walks over to the machine, unplugging everything, and sees that the device is already surging power at total capacity. Jalen then shoots 4 explosive darts at the machine, which only damages it slightly. Jalen then decides to put a whole ammo pack of the explosive darts onto the cloudburst, takes some steps apart from it, and fires another dart at the box. The box then explodes. It blows up the machine, and a blue explosion sweeps the whole floor clear, along with Jalen and Zion getting swept away. The machine's energy particles go all over the place on the top floor of the building.

The news helicopter swerves in the air and goes out of control, then eventually starts usually flying again.

 Jae gets blown back to the side of the building and hangs on to the side of the building. Jalen then climbs back up onto the floor and goes to find Zion and finds him under a whole bunch of rubble. He then gets Zion from out under the debris.

Zion then questions Jalen about saving him. "Why did you save me after everything that I have done?" Jalen helps Zion up off the ground, looks him in the face, and says. "It's because no matter what, I always choose to do the right thing; that's just who I am."

The building starts to become unstable from the explosion of the cloudburst. The installation in the building begins trembling and begins cracking and disassembling itself.

Zion shakes his hand and sucker punches Jalen. Zion then jumps out the window onto another building.

Jalen checks his thermal vision and sees that the building is empty. He then jumps out the window and lands on another building. Jalen departs from the scene of the destruction to go back to his grandfather and Maya.

The building starts to collapse into the plaza. The building crashes to the ground. The particles from the serum disperse across the city in the air and the water system across the town. The people in the crowd run back as far as possible to get away from the falling debris. Several minutes pass by, and Jalen finally arrives back at the office where his grandfather and Maya are waiting for him. When he walks in, Maya runs to him and hugs him. He immediately groans because of the injuries he has to withstand in his fight.

She says to him after realizing he's in some pain. "Jae, I'm so sorry I didn't even think about asking you how much pain are you in.

He then looks at her and faintly laughs. He then opens his mouth to reply to her saying. "It's okay. I'm just happy this is all over finally."

She then helps him into the training room to take off his gear. Bernard walks into the room afterward, and he just smiles at Jalen. He walks over to him and says to Jalen. "I just want to tell you I'm so proud of you, kid."

He then responds to Bernard with a smile and says to him. "Thanks, you grandpa but Zion got away."

"He's going to be back eventually, and when he makes a comeback, we will be ready," he then says to Jalen as he sits there in pain.

Maya goes and turns on the tv and switches to the news. There are images of the building collapsed on the ground on the information. A couple of people are being sent to the hospital. The news anchors start talking about the video from the news helicopter of Jalen and Zion fighting on the top floor. The news anchors start talking about who were those people. They even came up with a name for Jalen. The pictures and the video of Jalen were going viral under the name of The Emerald

Knight. Maya then walks over to Jalen to show him the title the city has given him.

Jalen then looks at the name and smiles, and says. "Not what I was expecting them to call me, actually."Maya looks at him and says. "Well, I wonder what made them come up with that name for you because I kind of like it."

Bernard then laughs and says to both Jalen and Maya, mocking the name their calling Jalen. "The Emerald knight is here to save the day."

The three of them all sit there and laugh, celebrating the big victory.

A couple of days pass by, and winter break is over. Jalen and Maya go back to school. Jalen goes to Maya's locker to speak to her in the morning. When he walks up to her locker, Justin runs up behind and jumps on his back.

He then says to Jalen after surprising him. "What's up, bro how was winter break without me?"

Jalen laughs and asks him. "It was actually pretty good for once." He then smiles and looks over in the direction where Maya is standing in.

Justin then turns and realizes what he was looking for, and he says to him. "Wait, did you two finally make it official."

He then looks at Justin, smiles, nods his head, and says. "Yeah, bro, her and I spent a lot of time together on the break. When did you even get back from your grandparents?"

He then responds to him and says. "We actually got back last night, and I crashed. As soon as I saw my bed, I still had to unpack all my stuff later when I got home.

Jalen laughs, and they walk over to Maya. Brea then walks up to everybody. The four of them all tart to talk about their winter breaks. Brea then says to everyone as she starts scrolling on her phone. "Damn, what happened in the plaza on New Year's Eve, and who is the emerald knight?"

Jalen and Maya look at each other, and he then replies to brea. "Yeah, it heard it was a lot of people that got arrested, and it was some explosion that happened on the roof. I don't know who the emerald knight is, though."

Brea looks at him and says. "Dang, all of that happened when I was gone."

Maya looks at her and says."It's crazy because I told my parents don't go out to the plaza too."

The school bell rings, and Maya closes her locker. The four of them all walk to their first period. They all have to walk into Ms. Jones's classroom for Algebra II. They all sit down at their desk and are well ready for class.

Zion returns back at his hideout and tries to find some medical stuff to patch himself up from his injuries from his fight with Jalen. He then sits down on a chair and says. "I will get my revenge on Jalen, fulfill my plan."

Bernard sits in his office space and gets many alerts around the city of people getting rushed to the hospital. He then sends Jalen an emergency text. He then gets a call saying that Jalen's little cousin is in the hospital, currently in a comatose state. The people in the hospital are getting tests run on their blood and seeing a high number of proteins in their systems. Some of them are showing very abnormal abilities while being under observation. Some people are showing strength, speed, flight, and other skills.

A couple of hours later, Jalen and his friends get dismissed from school. Jalen then tells his friends.

"Look, I got to run to my grandfather's real quick he said it's an emergency, so I'll probably catch up with y'all later, okay."

Maya smiles at him because she understands and says to him. "Yeah, go ahead and just text us later, Jae." Maya then kisses him, and he walks away to go to his car.Jalen then walks to his car and gets in it. As soon as he gets in, he looks at his phone and sees that his Grandpa text him, saying, meet me at the hospital. Jalen then leaves the school parking lot and drives to the hospital.

After a little bit of time, Jalen arrives at the hospital at the emergency room entrance and sees his Grandpa. Are then asks him. "Hey Grandpa, what's going on in here?"

He looks at Jalen and says to him. "There infected with something. I don't know what it is. I'm scanning everything to see. Jalen, you did destroy the machine, correct?"

He then looks at Bernard and says to him. "Yeah, I for sure did blow it up."

He then replies to Jae. "Was there any fluids left on the floor or splattered anywhere?"

He then responds to his Grandpa by saying. "I'm not sure; honestly, I didn't even think about checking. Wait, why do you ask, though?"

Bernard sighs and sucks his teeth out of frustration and says to him. "Look, be quiet, but I think the building falling within the plaza caused the serums particles to disperse around the city, and there's no telling what the actual radius was."

Jalen then sighs and says. "Well, what are we going to do then?"

Bernard looks at him and says. "We're going to do our best to help protect the city and these people."

Jalen smiles at his Grandpa.

Bernard then says to him. "There's one more thing, Jae, that you need to see."

Bernard and Jalen walk through the hospital and take him to Jalen's little cousin's room. The two of them stand outside the door because no one is allowed in the room at the current moment. The two of them then leave and go back to the office. When they get back to the office, they get an alert of a bank robbery that's seven minutes away. Bernard then looks at Jalen and says to him. "Hey, Jae, suit up."

Jalen smiles, throws his book bag on the floor, grabs his gear, puts it on, and says. "Grandpa put the location on my visor hud."

Jalen then goes up the stairs to walk out of the office onto the roof and then starts traveling from rooftop to rooftop.

Jalen then says to himself as he runs across the rooftops in the city. "I will be a beacon of hope and an object of justice to protect the city and its people no matter what and never give up on them. For they will forever call me The emerald knight." Jalen then dives off the roof and free-falls into the city.

The end

These characters will be returning soon……